I love Annie's body. It is strong and sensuous. She is feminine yet masculine, and over time she has become more butch. I love this about her, the way she can exude both sides of herself. Her strength and surety come back to me. I put my mouth on her nipples; they are hard like frozen blueberries, and she brings them to my mouth. I leave round, wet circles on her white gauze top. We are naked now. She holds my breasts in her hands, and we laugh. I say she is milking me, too long in Iowa, I say. We laugh softly, continuously. She turns me over and moves on top of me, working her way down my body with her mouth. How long will I last? This is always the hardest part — trying to last — I want her mouth on me for as long as possible. Her lips are thick, swollen. I feel her respond. I have never been with someone who has wanted me in her mouth more than she does; she has a hunger for it. Her mouth finds me — Oh God, her mouth.

LOOKING FOR NAIAD?

THE DRIVE

Trisha Todd

THE
DRIVE

Trisha Todd

THE NAIAD PRESS, INC.
1999

Printed in the United States of America on acid-free paper
First Edition

Editor: Christine Cassidy
Cover designer: Bonnie Liss (Phoenix Graphics)
Typesetter: Sandi Stancil

Library of Congress Cataloging-in-Publication Data

Todd, Trisha, 1961 –
  The drive / by Trisha Todd.
      p.   cm.
  ISBN 1-56280-237-2   (alk. paper)
  I. Title.
PS3570.03936D75   1999
813'.54—dc21   98-44748
                                                          CIP

For Kellee

Acknowledgments

I would like to express my deepest thanks to Barbara Grier for taking a chance on this book, and also to my editor, Christi Cassidy, for her help and advice. I would like to thank my good friends Don Alder and Sarah Lucht — Don for always keeping me in touch with my spirit and Sarah for helping me simplify the structure and the writing of the book. Thanks, guys!

My love to my family: Mom and Dad, Marci and Shelly. And especially to Shelly and Tom for letting me regroup in their room above the garage. Thanks to Jim for taking me in when I needed a place to hide. You're a good friend. My deepest gratitude to my very special students from Battle Ground High School — Joe, Megan, Heather, Antonia, and Justin — for inspiring me to act and write again. What can I say?

Deep thanks to all my friends at Vista Spring Café for keeping me working when I was not — especially Ted, Gary, and mostly Ben! You know I love you guys — you're family!

And all my teachers . . .

Finally, thanks to Landon for teaching me how to truly love. I love you, Buck!

And anyone else I may have forgotten . . .

"To worship freedom without growing,
is to end in bondage."

— Saint John of the Cross

THE DRIVE

Trisha Todd

SEPARATION

The night before I moved to Iowa I got scared. I don't think I had second thoughts. Well, maybe I did, but mostly I felt like I did when I was little and we would go swimming at the loody in Silverton, Oregon. I would stand on the rock ledge waiting to jump. It was cool there beneath the trees, cold when you stood there wet after swimming. To get there you would have to climb up the slick mossy rocks that hung out over the water; a constant stream of water kept it all moist and damp smelling, cool, a coolness so strong it runs all the way through your body, cleansing your mind and soul. Once you made it to the top you stood holding on to the tree and thinking about nothing more important than the jump. Down below everyone watched and waited for you to take the leap, so you couldn't wait too long. Sometimes it was okay to let others go before you, but you could only get away with that the first or second time. Then you were on your own. The bravest hung on to the rope after the first pass and dove in headfirst. I wasn't one of them. It was enough for me to jump feetfirst. But before you jumped there was the moment on the ledge. I would stand there with my heart pounding, paralyzed. I wanted to jump. I knew how it would feel to fall through the air and hit the water — the flight. But letting go was hard. The moment on the cliff before the jump was like a lifetime, the thoughts that ran through my head, the rush that went through my body.

That night in bed I felt the same. Little girl waiting to jump. When I finally took flight it was always the same, the freefall, the impact of landing, falling like a rock to the bottom of the water, and then the ascension to the surface. This was the moment that made it all worth it, the fight back up through the water after having been beneath the surface. I loved to hold my breath for as long as possible, in pools, in rivers, in lakes, in the ocean.

The water at the loody was cool and a deep green, the first layer warmed by the sun, deeper down, cool and dark. You would hit the water and descend, letting your body go as far down as your small weight would take you, then float to the surface like a dead fish. Then break the surface. After only one moment of relief, you'd climb up the rock cliff to begin again.

Over and over, all day long, all summer long — my whole life long. Climbing, jumping, hitting, descending, ascending, breaking through . . .

Water. I used to do the same thing in the bathtub. I would stay under as long as possible, watching movies I would run through from memory, listening to the silence, being born over and over again.

As I lay in bed I caught myself holding my breath, listening to the silence of my own thoughts, the movie of my own life being played out in front of me. Wondering how long until I surfaced.

I remember reading about women who killed themselves by drowning. Virginia Woolf. Kate Chopin's heroine from *The Awakening*. I thought this is how I would want to die, but how difficult it must be. Your body won't let you; it fights to surface, to live, to breathe. I don't know how they could accomplish this death — and I find it interesting that women are the ones who choose this way. Why? Maybe it is the desire to return to water; maybe it is the peacefulness of the death, the nonviolent aspect of it. It seems to me a Gothic death, a romantic expression of surrender.

I lay in bed, paralyzed, trying to pull myself together to brace myself for the big jump. Iowa. Iowa. I grew up on the ocean, and here I was traveling sixteen hundred and eighty-two miles, as far away from water as I could get. A world away. I feel like the first fish that attempted to walk out of the murkiness of the watery world it had been formed in. I wonder if my fins will turn into legs, if my gills will become lungs. Will my skin burn away from lack of moisture? When I touch myself I don't feel scales, just fine hair and skin. No, I am not a fish; I am just an animal lacking instinct.

This will be my third time driving to Iowa from Oregon, my first time moving there, though. Moving to Iowa. Moving to a new place, somewhere different. Where I could be different. Where I could start over. Where Annie and I could start over. A new birth.

Leaving the ocean was strange to me. I had always lived near the water — some body of water — and I had a hard time conceiving what this would be like. I decided to think of the cornfields as water. I didn't know if this would work, but it was worth a try. Leaving water far behind me. Not just water but the ocean, my identity. I have always been on one coast or the other; not being on the edge was new to me. For some reason, artists or "social deviants" tend to migrate to both coasts — something about living on the edge, perhaps. Whatever the reason, I was defying that. Iowa is in the middle, smack dab in the middle! Iowa is land, lots and lots of land. I will swim in a sea of land and open spaces, unprotected. The corn will be my coral, my seaweed. The birds like fish, me swimming underneath the surface of the sky. A mermaid in the corn.

One day I was teaching and I saw this quote. I really like quotes. This one fit, fit like skin. "A good traveler has no plans and is not intent on arriving," something like that. Lao-tzu from the sixth century B.C. I am reminded of this whenever I begin a journey, or when I don't think I am having one. It is not about arriving but about the trip there. The road. What we discover along the road. In Iowa there are many roads. Old country roads seldom traveled. Lao-tzu, I think, would like Iowa. He would definitely like the drive out there.

Iowa is mythical to me; not only is the place mythical, but the journey is also. I was moving away from what I knew and what was comfortable, into a place that was unfamiliar. But from what I know this is an important part of the journey. The Hero's journey anyway. The journey begins by separating yourself from your world and traveling into a dark and mysterious place. Granted, I was going to Iowa, not Hades, but the uncertainty is the same. There is a world out there. A world to explore.

In my uncertainty I create a story for myself, with myself as the Hero. The lone cowboy, the wandering sage, the Buddha by the river. I give myself all kinds of mythical personalities — and I will conjure them up when necessary. It isn't just a road trip; it is a vision quest, a symbolic death. I am diving into what Saint John of the Cross calls "the dark night of the soul," when the soul lets go of this world and goes into what to us seems like darkness but is actually a closer union with God. It is what my friend Nigel says is the *great paradox*: The deeper we descend into darkness or madness, the more detached we become from this world but the closer we get to God. We must let go of the world as we know it, all of our ties. A descent into the deep pool, submerged under water — in Iowa — then a surfacing.

I guess I tend to romanticize life. Okay, so I don't leave all my possessions behind. My laptop is securely tucked behind me in the back seat — I am going by car not foot; other than that I think the parallels are identical. I am in search of something. I am hoping I will find it in Iowa. I am looking for my purpose, my God, and my love. But no pressure . . .

When I was a little girl, my mom would pin my cape on in the morning and I was gone, gone for a day of adventure. Later it was my Bat belt and Bat mask, the accessories of superherodom. I could go all day living as Batman, then in the evening shed my cape as I shed that identity. I submerged myself in the waters of another. As I got older I traded my cape for a backpack and a journal; the forest behind my house became Greece, New York, L.A. Sometimes my cape became sex. I wore it freely and with confidence, but it was still a mask.

Amiri Baraka wrote a poem called "Why's/ Wise" in which he talks about losing your "oom boom ba boom." This is your spirit, and people want to strip you of it, and once it's gone it could take "a hundred years to get it back." It's all the same really — God and your "oom boom ba boom," that piece that makes you unique in all the universe. And it's this piece that keeps us afloat or drowns us.

In college, I heard about a scientist in New Jersey, Edward Witten, who was a physicist who believed that time travel was possible. His theory was that time is like a ball of yarn, the strands overlapping. That all time is just overlapping. I can believe in this theory because my life feels like a ball of yarn, structured to teach me a very important lesson, and until I "get it," the lesson just keeps repeating itself in slightly different ways, with slightly different people. "Why can't I get this!" I wonder. "Why can't I move on now?"

Sometimes I feel like I am sitting on the Dry Salvages; I had the experience but I missed the meaning.

Maybe time travel is possible by connecting to the music, the vibrating strings that make up everything, all playing the same song, but in a different key. Sound, the vibrating strings of time, the same dimension that the spirit world exists in — maybe this is the place where God lives? God is our song.

Six months ago Annie and I moved apart. Here I am moving to be with someone who had run from me six, almost seven months ago. How can I go back to what we both fought against, to what is unresolved? Something pulls me to her, yet keeps me protected at the same time. I feel like Frankenstein, running after my creator. It's as if everyone I have loved has run from me. At some point the finger points the other way and you have to say — me. Maybe it's me. But Annie is different. She is the shore pulling me toward her. The ocean has no choice but to meet the land; they are destined to meet — rhythmically calling to each other. Annie has always been this for me. She is the sun and I am Icarus.

So my angel and I are taking a trip, a journey to the land of Dorothy. To the middle of America. To this mythical place, Iowa. Iowa . . .

A student of mine liked to say that Iowa "did not exist," that it was "a conspiracy by the government." I thought about this. Did Iowa exist or not? For that matter, did Annie exist or not? So, maybe I was about to begin a journey to a place that didn't really exist to a person who was a myth I had created.

Annie is not Annie; she is "my Annie," the one I created, the one I need. Is she a dream? Nothing is very real. I read that everyone sees every color differently. Blue is not blue but rather our relationship to that color, which is tainted by our experiences. Every person sees everything differently. This is what saves us and gets us into trouble at the same time, I suppose.

Sometimes I wish that this nightmare of a year would end. I would wake up and my old life would still exist. I would be teaching every day, directing after school, my weekends filled with Annie and her son, Christian. I would see my students. Franky would bring me a latte in the morning and we would discuss our lives — and laugh. Franky could always make me laugh. But that is not how it works. The change and pain have all been for a reason — "the pain is part of the happiness," something like that. I have been in the "dark night" and some profound light will blind me! Right? At some point I will look back and know I made it through something huge. Right? But I have no perspective yet. I still believe blue is blue. In fact, what has been my nightmare could actually have been a wonderful dream to her. There's a thought . . . And maybe if I let go of it all as a horror movie, maybe then I can accept it. But I am still in the midst of it all; that's my fault, my choice. Still flailing around underwater, holding my breath.

Love is like drowning.

When I fantasize about death it is always by drowning — there is something sexual in that kind of death. Maybe it's the immersion of your body into something else — a total immersion, no air, no breath, no surfacing.

Do I really equate love with death?

Last night I dreamed about my cousin Rindy, who died of a heroin overdose almost two years ago after struggling with her addictions for years. In my dream I watched a video of Rindy before she died. She was looking into the camera and seemed out of it then, too, as if she was filming herself on drugs for us to watch. She seemed like a ghost already in my dream. When she overdosed she went into a coma and we gathered at the hospital for two days as she slowly left us. I remember my mom and her sisters crying together. My grandmother took Rindy's death the hardest. She worked at the state hospital with teenagers who had lost their minds and their lives to drugs.

Rindy's sister was devastated. She took the responsibility for her death on herself almost, thinking if she had been there she could have somehow prevented it, but it was a matter of time — Rindy devoured her addictions whole. I have a picture of all of us the day we went to see *Gone With the Wind* at the matinee in Silverton. In front of the Palace theater, all of us girls stood together in a row, arms around one another, each of us in these amazing time-capsule outfits. Colors God never intended to be in the same room together let alone stretched across an adolescent body. We all smiled broadly; we were quivering, vibrating almost, ready to be unleashed at the movies. The simple girlishness of the image lingers, the beauty of us. I guess there were demons already hovering over Rindy, demons that only a photo can disguise, a movie can change and make pretty. But in the snapshot, we were simply young girls like flowers waiting to bud. You can almost see the fairy light surrounding our innocence.

Death. It is winter, and winter has always been death to me. I don't know why I had this dream last night. Maybe it was an end of something, a reminder . . . Maybe just a note from another world: "Remember me?" Yes, I do.

* * * * *

Annie chose to move back to Iowa to be close to her family, so her son could be raised near his cousins and grandparents. So she could turn her life around and "do the right thing," not live a life that was against "God's will." God's will. I heard this a lot. I wonder what this means; obviously it means different things to different people. To a Christian it means one thing, to a Buddhist another; it is the difference that intrigues me. I have always had a hard time understanding the Christian God — not "God" or Jesus, both of whom I have faith in. I lack faith in religion per se — nothing has kept us farther from God, and especially Jesus. This fall I read a lot about Jesus and his years with the Gnostics. I learned much about him and his teaching, his mysticism. I began to see another man painted. Perceptions . . . I wonder how he saw blue?

Yet here I am moving into the center of the Religious Right. Iowa. I know there is something for me to learn there. If someone had told me ten years ago this is where I would be, I would have said, "You're crazy," but ten years is a lifetime.

I look at my key chain and I have two keys. My car key and the key to my storage unit. Two keys. Two. One year ago I had a handful of responsibilities, and they all had keys to them. But things are much simpler now. Two keys. I am thirty-six and people say my life should look different. I miss my handful of keys, my pockets weighed down by responsibility.

I have lived for six months in a loft — actually a room over a garage. My things are in storage, the things that have always given me comfort packed away until I find my way — until I find a home. Iowa?

I called Annie tonight, to find comfort. We don't do this well; we tend to fall apart on each other. Any doubt in one causes a chain reaction in the other, like dominoes. I wanted sympathy, she needed to hear strength — and so it goes. In all fairness, the roles have been turned around often. I hear the caged animal in her. The one that paces inside her cage. She tends to look at me as if I am on the other side, as if I am the one with the key, but I am not. I am in there too. We glare at each other as the door of the cage stands open. I am too sensitive, like a soft-shell crab.

Tonight I am saying good-bye. This is why I called. I don't say good-bye well — you would think I've had enough practice at it. I cry. I feel like crying now; somewhere I want to find comfort. Somewhere inside of me I want to find a home. I have traveled around the world to find a home, and I keep moving — sideways, crablike. I don't think that by moving I will find happiness. I know I won't. This must come from within. Yada yada . . . But I can't help trying. I can't stop myself from this relentless search, for someone — something — someplace — something outside of me, and yes, I do understand the significance in this, that my search must be turned inward, and I keep the lights on for as long as I can before I need rest from that journey too.

I will think of the sky like the ocean. Watch the

colors like a sunset on the beach. I can hang on to this.

I told Annie that when I moved back there I was going to write the "great American novel."

She said, "It figures you have to find some romantic reason for moving to the Midwest."

So many emotions run through my body. So many thoughts skitter through my head. I will miss my friends. I try to show my confidence in my decision, but I guess they see the doubt in my eyes and hear the nervousness in my voice. I can't hide much — it's pretty easy to read me. At least I think so. I am sure Annie senses this too, and it makes her feel responsible. Responsibility — this is something she fights.

The night before I leave I visit my friends Dean and Sydney — to say good-bye. David is there, my first acting teacher. They have so many questions. I don't hold up under the pressure; my emotions just keep leaking out. I can't stop crying. I am trying to convince them that this is a good thing, "an adventure," but soon I stop, because I don't really know why. I keep saying, "I don't know, but I have to go."

David says, "It's the drive. The journey is mythical."

Sydney says, "I guess you just have to go and see."

Dean says nothing. He is playing with two coins on

the table. He doesn't look at me, just sits there moving the coins around like a magician. Preoccupied with his game, I wonder which one to choose. I am also aware of his silence, but I don't dare ask. Sydney asks.

Dean says, "Unlike everyone else, I can't pretend to be supportive. Are you going to act in Sioux City?"

"Yeah, I think so. I don't know."

His brutal honesty undoes me. I am defeated by it. He doesn't stop at my tears, though. "I've been angry with you for a long time. I am so mad that you let others weaken you. Take you away from your goals. From your dreams!"

I've felt his disapproval before, but I've felt so much disapproval I learned to ignore it. But this I cannot ignore. It's funny; I almost didn't come here tonight. When I came to their door they weren't home yet. I sat on the steps, waiting for them. Sometimes I like to watch people enter places — these can be very private moments. Like when you go to the airport and you watch the people come off the plane. I never want to be seen first. You can see their preparation, their anxiety at the greeting. People reveal themselves in those moments. So I watch them arrive. I hear their recognition of me. Some moments have significance that we are usually unaware of at the time, but sometimes the heightening of our senses give us a clue that we will remember this, although we don't know why at the time. This was one of those moments. All my senses were keen. I noticed everything. It was cool, not cold. The porch boards slowly warmed under me. I sat on the steps with my legs apart, my fingers interlocked. There was the smell of wet pavement, moist soil, damp grass, winter voices, burning woodstoves... I would remember this. I saw myself sitting there. A nice shot for a movie. Me sitting, waiting, thinking, churning... All of it. Caught in a moment of transition. The moment on the cliff at the loody, poised, ready to leap.

I hear their voices before I see their faces.

Sydney is concerned I would not know to wait. She and I became friends during David's weekend workshops. We weren't close in school, but under David's wing we became friends. She uses her sarcasm as her cape, protecting the most fragile person I think I've ever met, an old soul with a frightened spirit. I found comfort in this; I understood her.

We did summer stock together in Ellensburg, Washington. Between rehearsals we would swim and lie in the sun. At night we would build campfires by the river, drink beer, and dance to Guns and Roses at the Best Western Motel. We didn't have much money; we didn't need much. It was one of my best summers.

I watched them approach.

"She'll wait," Dean said.

"I hope she waits. For God's sake, she'll know to wait, won't she?" David's impatience showed.

"I hope so." Sydney is usually in charge of these details. Pause. "What a great movie!'

"How brave of them. It was such a brave film. And oh, what brave performances!" David chimed in.

"I know!" Sydney said again, as if verifying the experience, making sure all saw blue as blue.

Dean was less than enthusiastic. He has always been the toughest sell.

Dean. My first college crush. My first college defeat. A twin soul, he is my Sebastian. Groomed to be a lumberjack, this blond boy from Clatskanie, Oregon, dreamed of being an actor. He modeled himself early after Robert Redford and at times his expressions are the same. Dean maintains a boyishness to him; only recently does he seem to have aged. He was aloof in sex, like he didn't need it, which made him a challenge for every woman and every gay man he met, but he remains almost unaware. I fell in love with him. We slept together once. It was nice. I was nineteen; he was twenty-seven, although he looked nineteen. I remember I felt safe and comfortable with him, but we were more like friends — or brother and sister.

Sydney moved in with him when I moved out. She had just had her heart broken too; we all bonded in our suffering. Their love started softly and sweetly, and they have been together ever since.

So there I sat, waiting to say hello to say good-bye. Perched. Watching the deep green pool below me. Hearing them talk of the movie they just watched. Thinking of the movie of my life. "I am brave too!" Did I say this out loud?

"I'm here. Here I am," I said. "I heard you guys coming up the street. Screaming your opinions of the movie. How was it?" Of course I already knew the answer, but I was buying time, making light, avoiding the reason I was there.

"Oh my God! It was just so brave." *Brave* was the word of the night, apparently. *Brave* summed up the experience.

"Oscars for the whole bunch," they all agreed.

I smiled. Inside I wished it was me in some movie they had just seen. I always wish this. I can never quite believe that it isn't. How odd life is. How unlike we thought it would be.

We hugged. Each hug was different, something attached to it, a breath of all the past in a moment. It was uncomfortable. I felt revealed, unable to hide my anxieties. I was wound tight. Something had to give.

The house is big and welcoming; every room is painted a different color. Sage, rust, blue. If I lived there I would live in the blue room, the room of creation, the artist's room, where Dean writes and bookshelves line the walls.

Dean made grilled cheese sandwiches, one at a time, but I had wine instead.

David glanced at me, but I couldn't hold his gaze. I blurted, "Oh, God I hate this! The defense of my life. I feel like I'm always defending some absurd choice I made that no one, and least of all me, understands. But here I go — make it convincing." I shifted but knew how to appear clear and sure. David was the first teacher whose lessons made sense to me. The Saturday mornings we met at his house laid the foundation for all I knew about acting. Maybe what I know of life. Good teachers transcend the classroom; they introduce the world outside.

He said softly, "You look clear and sure."

Good, I thought, I am. He had confidence in me. Confidence that I lack. But I act confident. "Yeah, you know, I'm just going to do it. Otherwise I'll never know."

The pressure kept up all evening, and I felt my defenses become thinner and thinner. The conversation evolved into a collage of "I don't knows."

Dean finally broke the monotony. "I miss your spirit."

Dean missed my spirit? I didn't know anyone knew it was gone. Asleep. Curled up in a fetal ball of protection.

Then he snapped, "You're a superstar."

I didn't know what he meant, yet I did. I knew something had been lost, not just with Annie, but a long time ago. According to my mom, I always acted. She says that even when I was very young, my best friend, Theresa, and I would put on plays in our garage. I don't remember this, but knowing it makes me happy, makes my life feel right. As I got older I spent time alone in my room taking myself on an emotional roller coaster. Teaching myself to cry on cue, forcing emotions in myself. I would leave my bedroom, my safe cocoon, and return to my family holding on to the secrets of myself. I was terribly shy at school, but acting brought me out of myself.

I said, "I can't get my feet under me, ever since I

did the movie. I lost heart. I've felt broken and defeated. Something happened then, something was lost, I know. Oh, God . . ." And I began to cry.

Dean reminds me of who I was, who I am. How I am still that person, but all I did was cry — like a baby, I couldn't stop. He told me he loves me, he has always loved me. I cried in his arms for a long time, told him I was scared and tired and alone — lonely. He told me again I am loved. I have been told this by others, but Dean is like a balm. Somehow I hear it from him. Suddenly I realized that the trip I thought I was taking is not the one I will take.

David's words reverberate in my mind: "Sometimes it's just about the drive."

Later that night I lay awake in bed for a long time. Images of my life shot like bullets through my mind as I lay there, touching myself to see if I was real. Trying to satisfy yourself can be lonelier than being with a lover. Failure brings the tears. Some of it is choice, some of it is lack of desire, but I am waiting. Waiting to explode with Annie, for Annie.

I met Annie almost four years ago during Christmas break. I was finishing up school, ready to go into my student teaching; Annie was in the middle of her second year of teaching biology. She lived in a small town about an hour out of Portland but had spent most of her life in Iowa.

The Christmas party was daunting. I didn't really know anyone, and I was forcing myself to go out and socialize during my break. I lacked friends in the gay community, least of all lesbians, but I wanted to change that. Lesbians made me uncomfortable because there was that added layer to friendships that made it stressful for me. It was as if every friendship was a potential relationship. There was no true clarity. I had enough problems with crossing over lines with straight girls, so why add to it?

I walked into the kitchen, and all I really remember was her coming toward me. She came to me like light — Annie's color is like gold, bronze. Her body is strong and long. She reminded me of Dominique from *The Fountainhead,* steel-blue eyes, tall, white-blonde hair. I stayed by her side all night. We talked about everything — growing up, our families, teaching, her son. Her eyes were so blue and clear. I was bathed in her light. It wasn't love at first sight, but I felt at home with her immediately. She was comforting. I was recovering from another love, and my heart was pretty much shut down. She seemed stable, like someone you could count on; as a friend used to say, she was "someone you could hang your hat on." I remember talking to my friends about her, saying she was stable, maybe even too settled for me. But something beyond her beauty lingered. Maybe the strings that compose us found each other, two parts of some song.

That night I took her hand and we went outside. Standing against the side of the house, I pulled her against me — we kissed, and we kissed again. She was firm against me, strong. We claimed each other. She came to me like a warm glow, slowly getting hotter — like clay softening in warm hands.

I called her a few days later and we had drinks. We sat in a gay bar in Portland at a small table against a wall and avoided looking into each other's eyes. We fumbled for something concrete to talk about. She wore faded blue Levi's, "worn," she said, "since high school." Those jeans fit like skin, ragged and weathered. They reminded me of a favorite sweater I'd had since I traveled through Europe. That piece of clothing summed me up. It was the same green color as my eyes, pieces of yarn coming undone, clumsily tied together so as not to unravel the entire sweater. The jeans personified Annie. They were her worn youth that barely fit. She also wore a black turtleneck sweater showing her navel, which was pierced. I began to see the inconsistencies then, the extremes I would come to know so well. We sat against the wall, nervously making conversation. First dates . . . I don't remember what we drank, but I do recall the silences.

Stealing another look at her, I asked her to come home with me to see the Christmas boats floating by on the river in front of my apartment. She agreed. There were no Christmas boats you could see from my apartment, but I guess that wasn't why she came home with me anyhow.

I made a fire and we stayed up late and talked,

mostly about God. She was a Christian, and I guess I wasn't prepared for what that meant. To me it meant a belief in God and Jesus, but this was all pretty vague to me. I had never met a lesbian — or any gay person, for that matter — who held on to such fundamental beliefs. I didn't understand how you could be a Christian and gay. But for Annie, to let go of one piece meant all the others might come tumbling down.

At that time I was against organized religion. For a while I considered myself a pagan, basically burning candles and sage and reading about white witchcraft. I told her all this. I guess we warned each other we were as far apart spiritually as possible. Now I can see how we both disregarded each other's beliefs, chose not to see the conflict from the beginning. A few months later, we began to understand the potential problems this could cause, but of course by then it was too late. I was hard on Annie about this. I hurt her with flippant remarks about what was most precious to her. I think I tried to wear her down, to reason with her so she would "get it." But it was me who didn't get it. She had faith in God, and I envied that. Threatened by her faith, I felt that I was fighting for her soul. Her family and her religion clearly didn't include me. I saw it as a battle, and if I lost I would lose her. She never really knew that her faith was what made me love her; it was what I needed to bring me back to God. In the war between us I felt God's presence in my life again.

Before any of this became our obsession, it was all

exciting and wonderful. At one point that night I changed into something more comfortable, and she asked me if she could too. This was a moment that years later I would remember. I knew then I liked her — a lot. I liked that she felt comfortable with me. I can still see her walking down the hallway from my bedroom in my favorite white V-neck T-shirt that was so worn it was almost transparent. It hung against her body like a sheer gauze curtain. She smiled at me as though we both knew then that we liked each other. I knew she would be my friend. That was all I knew then, just that I really liked her — and hoped she liked me. All very simple. We complicate it all so much. I liked that there wasn't a sexual push right off the bat. She was soft, sweet, and I could tell she was real. She was a nice girl from a nice family who had a nice life. She was someone I could make a home with.

I didn't know if I should make the first move, or allow her. I later found out she was waiting for me, since I was the hostess and all. She sat on the couch; I sat near her on the floor. I took her foot in my hand as we talked and I rubbed it; I wanted to touch her, but I was cautious. I felt nervous because then I knew it was up to me. I sat up and kissed her, then pulled her down on top of me. She spent the night, but I didn't think we would make love. I wasn't ready. I didn't push it. But she had other ideas.

True, there were no Christmas boats that night, but I swear I saw lights.

* * * * *

The waves of memories crash. I toss and turn. I am still the little girl waiting to jump off the cliff at the loody, in Newport riding bikes with Theresa, clamming with my father, watching my mom hang the clothes on the line, smelling the fresh sheets like dried seaweed underneath me all night. It's as if I'm still there, lost in the fairy colors of summertime, picking strawberries with my sisters, sweet peas with my mom, playing with favorite cousins Donny and Mark at the loody, building forts at Grandpa and Grandma Wagner's. Christmastime with all my cousins, my whole family, driving in cars — away from places and to places, back and forth. I miss me as a child. As a tomboy. My life of summers, and water.

My grandmother once told me she always knew I was different. My mother had said the same thing. When finally at age thirty I told my dad I was gay, he said he thought he always knew — but "he just wanted me to be happy." They said the same thing when I told them I was going to Iowa, but I could tell they were weary of my moving.

Every Christmas, my father took us all out to chop our own tree down. We went up an old logging road through the snow with steep dropoffs on either side of us. My mother would be so frightened she would make us lie on the floor of the car while my father laughed at her fear. This was a game at our house. My dad would find a snake or a mouse and chase my mom into the bathroom with it. She would refuse to come out, and my dad would just laugh. Once a snake made its way into our house while my dad was at work. It was summer, so the doors were open and we were all home from school. My mother made my sisters and me all climb up on the kitchen counters and sit there to escape the ferocious garden snake. Then she had me climb down and bring her the phone to call my father to come home and capture the snake. Of course I was completely freaked out and scared to death, but I wanted so desperately to be the hero that I even tried to capture the snake myself but couldn't. I was too afraid, I couldn't conquer my own fears. I felt I let her down.

My mother grew sweet peas along the sunny side of our house. During the spring and summer when they were in bloom, my mom would place a small vase of flowers next to our beds. Once a week she washed our sheets and would hang them outside on the line to dry. At night you could feel the crisp seaweed sheets, smell the sweet peas, and hear the ocean. I never wanted to leave Newport. I was deeply happy.

Remembering Newport can still bring tears to my eyes. When we moved from there I cried and swore that someday I would return. I would move back and live on the beach again. Ever since then I have returned to the water and felt most at home there. And now I couldn't be moving farther away. Into the middle of the country, into the desert, away from what I know. With someone who may not even want me.

Just remember: "The corn like the sea, the corn like the sea ..."

* * * * *

The moon is bright outside my window, it seeps
into my bed in the loft. Outside the air is calm, still.
It is quiet. I look at the phone as if by noticing it will
ring. As if Annie will feel my need through the night,
seventeen hundred miles away. Should I call? No. I
want to wait. Besides, after our earlier conversation
she must need some space. I told her I was scared and
nervous, but she didn't want to deal with it. What is
she doing tonight? Is she missing me? I huddle in the
warm bed, pulling the covers close to my face. I am
cold. Maybe I won't go. Maybe, in the morning,
instead of packing I will unpack and stay. Maybe I
should call Annie and tell her I'm sorry, but I don't
feel good about this, especially after my night with
Sydney, Dean, and David. Dean's words ring; my eyes
are still swollen from my tears.

I can't sleep. I have been running — backward.
Images like the world seen through a car window rush
past me. I don't want anyone to know I'm afraid. I
want them to have confidence in my decision to go, to
see what's on the other side. To go into the dark
forest looking for the fairies.

My sister Lynn helps me pack my car. I don't have
much. I want to simplify. Lynn is much more
organized than I am; both my sisters are very together. I feel like a hurricane in their presence. Lynn

takes her time, packing methodically. I tend to throw things in. With her help it all fits nicely. I take only what is necessary. I packed clothes, a few select books, candles, papers I may need, the computer, my easel, some music, Christmas presents for Christian and Annie. And I bring my TV, which is larger than anything else. It is my own leviathan! It is black and reminds me of the black holes in space. It is too big, far too big. But since it has been my friend for the last four months, my company in the loft, it too has earned the right to journey.

We laugh as we load. This trip after all isn't real. I am only living a scene in a movie. The cameras follow me — they are neutral, objective. Maybe they show something that I can't see; maybe if I watched I could see my life from a distance and then I would know. I would have some insight.

December twenty-eighth. Sunday.

I say good-bye to Lynn. This is hard. She has helped me so much. She is apprehensive about the move but knows I have to go. I don't want to cry. I cut it all short to avoid the tears. I hate those. I hate to say good-bye. She understands. She hates this moment too.

The ritual — coffee. Coffee for the drive. Essential. It is both fuel and entertainment. It offers the traveler a task. Too much, though, and you descend to the other side. But when you drive this is the drug of choice, and normal boundaries are meant to be stretched. The seasoned traveler even looks forward to the bad truck-stop coffee. Like the cowboy's harsh whiskey, this sort of coffee causes the mouth to contort. A vocal release that sounds part pain, part relief issues forth: "Aarrahhh!" Shift in your seat — pedal to the floor — turn up the music — get serious we are on a drive —

Get serious, I tell myself.

I take to the road. I am scared and excited. Everyone I know has told me they hope this works, but they are nervous. I take this with me. I am alone now. I stop at the gas station and hand him my credit card. It is denied. If this were a movie the audience would mumble collectively, "Don't go." But I am the character that fails to see the signs. This may be my tragic flaw. I pay cash and go deeper into the forest.

INITIATION

As I drive out of Portland I begin to feel alive. I am going to my love after all. On the other side she waits for me. The drive is freeing, yet I am trapped in my thoughts — they are all I have, and I begin to see that this forest is within me. My doubts and fears bob inside me — I am like a fish on a line, being reeled in, yet I want to fight and be free. I can't escape now. She never called the night before, and this haunts me. The signs have been clear. Annie has given me enough to know this move is too much. My presence in her life there will be too much. Maybe I have forced her? Maybe it is her fear of losing me and not her desire to have me that motivates her? Down deep I know I am headed for a fall.

I flip on the radio and suddenly remember Palm Springs. It was unforgettable. The weather was pretty good, except for the day we went to Joshua Tree and it actually snowed on us! We had parked at a campsite up in the mountains and sat in the Jeep with the snow falling all around us. We drank wine out of Dixie cups, ate cheese and bread, and fell deeper in love. I took a picture of her in the Jeep as she drank her wine with snow in her hair and happiness in her eyes. She took a picture of me at the wheel, sunglasses on and smiling. It is me as only she knew me. I have another picture of us swimming together in the pool, our arms wrapped around each other's necks, two waterlogged lovers. When everything is new, anything that happens is a beautiful memory.

We sat by the pool every day, started drinking gin and tonics around ten in the morning, laughed and swam. Around two we would go into the house and make love, nap, then go have lunch, shop, come home and sit by the pool, swim, and drink more gin and tonics. In the evening, after a wonderful dinner, we would sit in the hot tub looking up at the stars and the mountains so very close, watching the stars shoot and fall. We made love every morning, every afternoon, every night. Our warm skin against each other was healing to the cold we had felt in Oregon. Burnt skin — hot, sweaty bodies gliding over each other. We trusted each other with our hearts then, held each other's in our hands.

In Palm Springs we stayed with old friends of mine. They asked us questions about our relationship, trying to figure out just where we were going and what we wanted from each other. They asked us what we fought about, and do you know we were stumped? We had never fought. We looked at each other, trying to see what we could possibly find in the other to disaprove of. They laughed at our innocence; we shook our heads at their cynicism, turned toward each other and dove into the pools of color we both sought. We knew there would be things that we would disagree on but nothing that would challenge our love. The beginnings are always so incredible, so soft and intense. So careful and carefree, and so fleeting.

We couldn't keep our hands off each other. We were very territorial, and when we went out together we saw no one else. From the very beginning we kept our eyes on each other when we were out in public, as if we were both afraid of what space and distance may bring on. I trusted her because I would watch her in the bars and she didn't seem to see anyone else, only me. I must have known this was not real, but I didn't want to lose that trust and confidence in us. We would dance in the evenings and drink tequila. At one bar we made love on the pool table in a secluded room as the regulars sang along to the jukebox on the other side of the wall.

She talked to Christian every night, but at that time I didn't understand the need. I do now. She felt a lot of guilt; there was a sadness deep inside her, and regrets about his first year or two of life. When he was a newborn, she gave him to her parents to raise, and only after a month did she know she wanted him, that she was willing to make the sacrifice. She never dreamed that she would live a gay lifestyle and raise her boy in that atmosphere. She had told herself that when the time came it would only be a matter of stopping, finding the right man, and marrying. She wanted to offer Christian another life than the one she had lived. She thought she found it with me, that I was secure, responsible — and solid.

The second time we went to Palm Springs, Annie and I knew each other much better. We were more comfortable, at home with each other, and we could relax. Again we drank our gin and tonics, ate bagels, lay in the sun, and talked. We sat by the pool and read a play together, playing all the parts. Something new came out of her during this; she confided that she really always wanted to act. Maybe here was a place we could connect again, but it wasn't to be. Oh, sure, we shopped, ate out. One night we went dancing, drank tequila and danced all night, then we came home drunk and made love on the carpet, laughing. But there was a darkness she brought with her to Palm Springs; something had changed.

"Stop! Look around you. Notice the world. Stop going under." This is my conversation with myself. I have to keep myself above the surface. It is a fight.

I love driving through the gorge. When the wind hits the Columbia, you can see the whitecaps on the water. Once I thought of opening a small restaurant out here, a little inn. But now I realize how long ago that was. Only fifty miles into my trip and already it seems the real journey is much farther along. I went into the gorge once with this guy I was in love with at the time — or so I thought — and he took me up to the observatory and over to the Maryhill Museum for the first time. We went to the Stonehenge war memorial and I performed Lady Macbeth for him while standing on the altar as the sun was just rising. "Spiritus Mundi"? The summer before I met Annie he came to my apartment once. He had been painting and living in South America in the rain forest and he came upon a tribe that thought he was Jesus. We talked as we paddled his boat out into the river. A butterfly landed on his shoulder during a ritual; to the tribe this was a sign. For him too. He believed he was Jesus. Maybe that's who I've been searching for? Maybe that's what I see in Annie?

I need another cup of coffee . . .

Palm Springs. Palm Springs . . . The place where we fell in love, stayed in love, and realized our love was in trouble — at least for that one spring, last spring.

I try to listen to *A Tale of Two Cities,* but I can't concentrate. I listen to *The Hero With a Thousand Faces* instead. I decide this is a metaphor for my trip. I guess I need to make it profound and romantic, not stupid and pathetic.

The tape keeps playing; I hear pieces of it. About the Hero needing to separate, go through an initiation, then return. The separation can be a calling, a luring, or it can be voluntary. Once gone he then encounters "a shadowy presence that guards the passage." From there the Hero goes into the "dark kingdom" or faces some battle, then descends into death. Within this initiation he encounters many obstacles, tests or helpers. His victory can be represented by sexual union, atonement, or his own divination. Finally he returns to the world. If he remains blessed he becomes a teacher; if not he flees and is pursued. I feel like this Hero. Or maybe it's true what Annie says, that I just need to romanticize everything I do to give it meaning. She doesn't know that I want to let go of this dark fog too. I want out too. I feel trapped too. I want to be rescued too.

I stop for gas in Kennewick. It is ninety-nine cents a gallon. I can't believe it! These are carloads of people, on all their own journeys, stopped here, like purgatory. Music is piped in and the wind blows so hard I feel like I could fly, given a cape. All stopped here for gas, lined up, all on a trip somewhere. The station has cameras so you can't pump and run. You're safe with me, I think. I don't feel very lucky. In fact I feel that the bottom will drop out.

I realize I'm talking to myself, thinking out loud as I pump my gas, and that is why the man pumping next to me looks and wonders. This just makes him pump faster.

"The road will do this," I say. "Too much time spent alone and thinking. Bad combination."

"Fourteen fifty-five," the woman says from behind the counter.

"Hmm? Oh yes." Caught again, I pay, gather my treats, and head deeper into the forest of my thoughts.

I brave the wind, my imaginary cape flying behind me as the man in the next island watches me enter my capsule. They call gas pumps *islands*. I understand this all too well. My island is slowly sinking, but the wind catches my sail and I am off.

I eat lots of beef jerky, drink coffee, nibble sunflower seeds. The food of car journeys. It reminds me of the car trips I would go on with my family. My sisters and I would try to see who could make her jerky last the longest. Usually I would win, but it was an empty win. I sucked my beef jerky until there was no flavor in it; an hour later mine would still be intact while theirs was long gone. Mine would be all white and anemic looking — just flavorless flesh — while they had long forgotten the game. Maybe I do this with relationships. Suck them dry. Leave them white and flavorless. Try to make them last as long as possible, longer than anyone else in her right mind would. I eat it quickly now. It makes me sick, but the chewing takes away some of the boredom.

Cars and road trips meant time for Annie's family to talk and sing together. Her parents were missionaries in Holland. I was jealous of her religious beginnings. The strong foundation that was laid. Jealous that mine was not inherited, but blessed that I have had to find my own way. Hers was learned, mine was found. I don't guess either is better; each has its moments, each has its emptiness.

I went to church when I was little, but it really had no meaning. The experience never followed us home, and I wondered why we went. At one point we stopped. I sensed a great relief on everyone's part. No more church! But then something was missing, some piece. Annie had this piece. Her family taught her of God from the very beginning, but when she got older her relationship to him didn't fit theirs. Her relationship to him then became one of extremes, either all good or all bad. There was no *lukewarm*. Mostly I think she felt she didn't measure up. I think this would be the worst, to believe in a God that doesn't approve. I guess it would be like having a father who witholds his love.

Cars have had different memories for us. It seems we have both spent a lot of time in cars.

Annie. For her, travel was a group event. She and her family traveled around the countryside in a VW, spreading the gospel and Bibles. They lived in communes with others who had the same vision. One place she lived was an old castle with high ceilings, big sliding double doors, and lots of rooms. The nursery had a tunnel that went for a quarter of a mile and came out into a concentration camp behind the castle in the woods. Mysteries and secrets. Places to hide. Annie even promised me tours of the hidden places with her as my guide.

"Yes. I will take you some day! I can't wait..." she would say with light in her eyes, as if this place was her own sacred grove. I like to think of her, this innocent little blonde-haired girl spreading the "good news," living in Holland, and rolling her own cigarettes since fourth grade.

Annie would tell me about her car trips, and I was envious. They would sing and play games, while my sisters and I would fight over space. On our family vacations, my stomach would feel sick; we were all too close in that car. But I could separate from my family and she couldn't. Her family would not let her go. My parents always let me fly on my own, for instance. This was hard on my mom, but she knew it was right. Annie's mom never let her go, still hanging on to her, making it harder for Annie to fly, too much weight on her back.

I think about Annie and hold myself close. In another day or so I will see her, touch her, smell her, taste her ...

On our first trip to Iowa, Annie and I stopped to attend a family reunion in Minnesota. We had decided to rent a car because my convertible was too old and iffy, her Jeep too cramped. Christian was small enough to lie in the back window like a stretched-out cat. We doubled as a suburban family in that new Taurus, as sure of each other as we were of that car. In Minnesota she took me out to the cornfields and made love to me on a little dirt road. We made love surrounded by tall stalks of corn that served as a wall of protection. She had promised that moment before we left. She couldn't wait to show me the corn and wheat, to have me hear my first thunderstorm and see my first firefly. We stayed on a lake in a little cabin. The last night we were there a thunderstorm rocked us. We were in a little cabin on a lake in Minnesota with a thunderstorm that roared inside us both. It was exciting lying next to her and feeling the thunder in my belly, in my bones. I felt safe with her. We were a family then, a whole life ahead of us.

Traveling with Annie felt natural to me. I learned to like it early on. The mythology of it must vibrate on my strings. I am not the first to be called to it: For the wandering Bedouins, "travel is travail," and the medieval Japanese believed that the sorrows of travel were meant to be transformed into poetry and song. The road is not meant to be smooth. I had been moving my whole life. The first ten years I was planted. Once the roots are pulled it's hard to feel the solidity of the ground.

I spent the first ten years of my life in Newport, Oregon. My dad was the mayor of Newport. In 1968, when Bobby Kennedy came through for the Presidential election, my dad took me to the airport to meet him. He was my hero at the time. I had a poster of him in my room while my sisters had Jack Wild and the Beatles. The poster said: "Some men see things as they are and say why. I dream things that never were and say why not." At the airport my father lifted me on his shoulders and I shook Bobby Kennedy's hand. He was young and beautiful, full of tomorrow. In restaurants along the waterfront, there are many pictures of him from that time. He is always walking along the beach, barefoot with his white pants rolled up, a smile on his face, and his long unkempt hair blown by the wind. He is looking out into the ocean and his eyes seem sad yet strong. There are people around him but he always seems alone. He was a picture of a romantic leader to me, mythical. Two weeks later after the California primary, I sat in front of the television early one morning while the rest of my family was asleep, and I watched him gunned down right in front of me on the screen. I will never forget the moment I shook his hand, and the moment I sat alone and watched my hero killed.

Still and all, I loved our life, the ocean's roar constantly in the background. My mom hated living there because she said it rained all the time. But the water was salty and we were forever bathed like sea mammals, kept moist — like living in a tide pool. My father would bring home fresh salmon and crabs. It was so cheap then that we ate crab Louis for dinner and razor clams for breakfast. I remember Dad taking me clamming before dawn, taking me into the early-morning diner with the other fishermn, having coffee and breakfast as we discussed tides and how the clams were running. The night still hung over us, the night and fog, as we would finally make our way to the beach, looking for small air bubbles in the sand. Like balloons they would emerge and we would chase them, chase them because the bubbles meant the clams were close beneath the surface of the sand. My dad would shovel with his clam shovel as fast as he could, then I would pick out the clams quickly before they burrowed back down into the sand. I loaded our kill into a bucket. At home we cleaned them, then Mom breaded them and cooked them up for us for breakfast. Fresh and from our hand. I loved our life there by the ocean, in our house that my grandfather built.

My dad named me after one of his sisters who died of cancer. He always said I reminded him of her. I hardly remember her. When I think of her all I see is her in her hospital bed smiling. She was dark like him with those high Indian cheekbones that distinguished all of them as a family. It is what distinguishes me too, I guess. But the memory of my dead aunt, one in a long line of brothers and sisters my father lost, must be imprinted on him in ways I can't begin to know. I think this is why he keeps a bit of a distance from those around him. It's not a coldness but a distance that sometimes makes you wonder how to get close to him.

My dad is handsome and strong and sensuous. During the summer he loved to swim, and it is because of him we sought out perfect swimming holes in which to cool off during the hot summer days. We would pack a lunch, pack our dog, and head off in our car in pursuit of the best place to swim. My mother was less adventurous; her role was not to explore but to settle. I learned his love for exploring. But my dad was never really prepared for our adventures. Once he took us all out deep-sea fishing. My mother of course expressed her concern over every obstacle or problem we might encounter, but my father simply laughed at her fears. We had not even made it out of the bay when the boat began to sink. We eventually made it back in some unmemorable way. But I do recall us standing on the dock watching the boat my father had borrowed sink into Yaquina Bay. My mother's face was full of "I told you so"; my dad looked somewhat defeated, somewhat whimsical at the irony of it all. He taught me to shrug my shoulders at sinking ships. My father never gave up, though. We were forever following him on some little adventure that he had envisioned.

I have a picture of my parents in my mind. We were living on the beach then, and it must have been summertime. My parents were standing out in our garage. He had his arms around my mom and flowers in his hand. They were kissing a long, sweet kiss of apology and forgiveness. I watched that moment. I knew it was private, but I watched out of wonder and happiness. My parents were private with their affection, but in that moment I had a glimpse of something essential, perhaps what held them together. They were married so young, sixteen and eighteen; they grew up together. They have been partners in all they have done, each sacrificing for the other, letting go of individual dreams for some collective one that seemed obscure to me.

It is ironic. I never saw my parents fight, but I always knew when they were not getting along. There was silence. And it was always my mom whose silence ran deepest. Annie watched her father beat her mother up. But the person she related to was her dad, despite his wrongdoing and fighting for space. I watched my mother go inside herself for comfort; she never seemed to ask for it. At some point in our relationship, almost a year ago, Annie and I sought help from a therapist, but we were too angry to hear anything from anyone. Our therapist told us we had married each other's mother; we learned and became the roles we had been shown. Annie became her father; I became her mother. I was my father; she was my mother. Playing out each other's scripts, she said.

I can't wait to see Annie. Maybe my fears will go away. I wonder what she's doing. How is she preparing for my arrival? *Is* she prepared? Am I? Who is this new friend she talks about? This one who she can be "immature" with. When she told me about her, I got nervous. I had memories to remind me of what that may mean. "Someone to be immature with." Have our lives drifted so far apart? Can we still connect? Can we survive her parents, her family, her world?

I have this daydream as I drive: I arrive and her parents are at Annie's house. They are upset with my being there; they will not allow this. I have invaded their world and the perfect picture may be exposed for what it is. They offer me money to leave; Annie doesn't say anything. I want to take the money because I have none, but I can't because of my pride. Her father hands me the money; I tear it up. I walk out. I drive home.

I pray to God. I wish I felt cradled by God.

* * * * *

46

Annie is the only one who understands the two of us. Everyone else is disappointed. This ties us together. Dean's words ring. "You are loved. You are a superstar!" The words make me feel like I am strong again, as if in them there is something that was lost, but it is not found. I am just reminded of the loss. He told me last night that he missed my "spirit," like my spirit was dying. I feel my spirit dying as I drive. What am I feeling? Why do I feel like this? Last night when we talked Annie seemed so distant, angry that I had called, that I was feeling sad and nervous. She was on her way out with her friends. I thought she would call me later, when she got home. I lay awake, hoping for some touch from her.

"Yes, Dean, my spirit is dying. It is dying because I feel my love slipping from me. But I will soon be there, and I will capture your heart again, Annie. I will make you love me. I will show you I am enough, and I will be happy there. I will write and paint and love you. We will cradle each other."

There is a rest stop between Ritzville and Spokane. Annie and I have stopped here every time we have taken this trip. It is beautiful in the summer — hot; in the winter it is bone chilling. It is everything it should be. We have taken long pauses in our drives here. Christian has played and Hana, our dog, has run; we have stretched and looked out on the land. There is a lake down below. In the summer it is inviting, and you can practically smell the coolness of the water; now it is frozen. Everything here is either dead or asleep. I like standing on the bluff, looking out over the valley. I think of my sister Morgan who, when we drove into Prineville, always thought of Indians on horseback looking out at the valley below them. I think of this now; it's a good shot in my movie. I'm standing on the bluff; cut to Indians; cut back to me. The throughline must be Indians, Sioux City, then Oregon, me, Indians.

When you drive through Washington, somewhere between the tri-cities and Spokane, there is a monument to wild horses. They are perched up high off the road. You have to look for them. Christian couldn't wait until we got there; we would look up on to the hills and see the wild horses made out of metal, running with their manes flying in the air. But they are caught; frozen, suspended — mid-flight. They are beautiful! Maybe he thought we were like the horses running.

The rest area is under construction, so I go into the portable toilet. During Christmas Annie sent cards to my two sisters and my mom and dad, saying that she would never leave me alone in Iowa; I think of this while I pee in the cold eastern desert of Washington.

I make a mental list of the best and the worst places for my car to break down. I think of the best and the worst places for me to have a breakdown. My car gets Spokane; I choose Wyoming. I pull my pants up in the hard plastic cubicle on the bluff overlooking the valley below, then open the cold brittle door and reenter the world. I feel invisible again. But I do see people entering the warm and modern restrooms. I am the only one who used the portable. Back in my car again, I wish desperately that I had already arrived. In front of me are the mountains; they are all that lie between Annie and me. Mountains and prairie . . . Lots and lots of prairie.

There is snow on the ground and ice on the water. I wonder what the weather will be like in the mountains. I have new chains; I feel confident. Actually I am excited to be prepared for something — I am prepared for snow and ice. In the back I have a sleeping bag, just in case I get stranded. My mom wanted me to bring this sleeping bag.

"You never know if there will be a storm." My mother's voice is as loud as if she were sitting next to me in the empty passenger's seat. This is the storm my mother has been waiting for her whole life. The one that occurs in the mountains every weekend. The one she feels safe from, yet haunted by.

They say a candle is good too. It can actually keep the inside of the car warm. The heat of *one* candle. I wish I was as prepared for the other breakdown. No candles, sleeping bags, food, or water can save me from that.

My one key taps against my leg.

* * * * *

49

I stashed some cheese in the trunk, the cheese I brought for Annie's family. Annie always brings cheese when she goes home; it's what her family most misses from Oregon. That and the ocean — but I can't bring that. I must be deluded or just a romantic to believe that three loaves of Tillamook cheddar will heal my place in their world, that when they get the cheese their hearts will melt and they will embrace me and welcome me into their family. The cheese will be the bridge — and I will be cradled by them. This makes me smile and cry as I drive across the Washington–Idaho border.

"I could always eat the cheese if I get stranded by the storm," I say matter-of-factly, as if my mother were sitting there next to me.

* * * * *

Every once in a while I sigh as I drive. The sighs are heavy, the kind of sighs you sigh as you get ready to jump into the loody. This is the collage of my happiest memories: my cousins, staying with Grandma and Grandpa Wagner on their farm, marionberry cobbler, forts, barns, old quilts, old houses. Across the road was the loody; a half mile up the road was the A&W. Grandma and Grandpa had a big red barn, a huge garden, a goat and chickens, and a hill to explore. Everything a child needed to fill every moment of summer. Herbal Essence shampoo, root beer floats, strawberries, blueberries, playing outside until we were so tired we collapsed on the floor of the living room; waking up excited, running downstairs to start the day. The cool dewy mornings, the hot thick air of the afternoon. All of this comes back to me now.

The six of us built a fort with pieces of wood we found in the old barn. We made hammocks out of burlap sacks and hung our small brown budlike bodies from the strong boards straddling the walls we had so carefully built. Here my spirit was alive. I think of the picture my mother painted of us swimming in the loody: We wore old hats we had found at the farm, painters' hats we wore even when we swam.

It was the last summer I got to be myself, undefined. I was ten. Free from sex and relationships. After that summer I became a girl. I knew that summer was the end of something that I was not ready to let go of. It was time to become someone else. No one told me this, I just knew it. And I mourned. I knew enough to be sad, that something — some part of myself — was over, some new me was beginning. I began to disconnect from myself after that. I tore Batgirl away from me, put her in a box in my closet only to be taken out by myself, alone. My body changed. Outside I had shed a skin and was about to be reborn as someone else, someone I wasn't ready to become, but someone my body was forcing me to be. A butterfly or an abortion, depends on how you see it. Perceptions. She still haunts me, the little girl. She is the one I see sitting next to me now.

* * * * *

My car is silver and I imagine I am a superhero. I have always imagined this. I can't quite come to terms with the fact that I am not. I believed it for so long. When I was little my mom would pin a towel on the back of my shirt in the morning and the whole day I was able to fly because I had a cape. I dreamed I could fly; I knew that if I tried hard enough I could. I used to have dreams, vivid dreams, where I would fly. The whole dream was about me flying. Taking off and flying. I felt it. I know what it is like to have flown. I was always aware I had failed because I couldn't fly in life, because I had felt it in my dreams. Sometimes the dream is more real.

I know someday I will fly.

Sometimes driving is like flight. The sleeping bag is like my cape. My mom always made sure I had a cape. Maybe I maintain this seeker in me because she is the little girl at the loody. Free and full of possibilities, she is in me, I am still her, but changed — altered slightly. Isn't it odd how our spirits don't change? How God creates us, we are his creation, and what is written on us is who we remain, no matter what. I can't seem to lose her. That summer I had to grow up, but I couldn't lose her. She got stuck there in the moment between two worlds. Like the fairies; a personal spiritus mundi.

There is someone with me in the car, someone sitting next to me. My angel. He must be near me.

God says, when you are most alone that is when he is near. He must be sitting next to me holding my hand because I feel so alone. He should be cradling me now. I am in the mountains. It is snowing, but the snow isn't sticking. It is dirty, wet snow. White and muddy. I feel that if I make it through these mountain passes I am home free. I will not need the chains. The mountains in northern Idaho are beautiful, but they are full of white supremacists. This is so weird to me. How could something so beautiful be speckled with evil, dark-hearted people? I wonder if I have ever met a truly evil person. Annie says they exist, but I don't know that I have ever met one. Maybe my angel has protected me.

Maybe.

When I drive I like listening to talk radio. It is like the mountains of Idaho, though, speckled with hate.

Sometimes I feel Christians are like this too. Beautiful mountains speckled with hate. Like snow dusting the dark earth underneath, dirty white snow.

Maybe the cheese will help.

I always hurry as I drive through northern Idaho. My fear is probably ridiculous, but I feel something here I can't explain. I remember when my former girlfriend Jesse and I drove through here she had something in the car that made me think of others she had been with. I threw it out the window. We laughed about it later. What would the white supremacists think when they found this purple love tool on the side of the road?

I remember staying in Saint Regis, but I don't remember who I stayed there with. Jesse or Annie? Maybe both. I must be hard to love. I don't trust people. I am attracted to those who are untrustworthy, or maybe it's me — yes, that's right, it's me. I'm the one. But I'm learning the other side now. "The Green-Eyed Monster" — maybe this is me. I don't let people close to me, so they are driven away by my isolation. I don't know how to let people in. Annie told me that either I'm far inside myself or I'm forcing myself into someone else. In everything I do, I push too hard. It's a joke in my family. Morgan says I go at everything "like I'm killin' snakes." When I walk I stomp. You can hear my footsteps all over the house. Sydney used to give me a bad time about how noisily I was making my tea in the morning. I am not very delicate. Annie says when I eat tacos it isn't pretty. I can't help it; I devour things. It is what has helped me and hurt at the same time. It has given me my drive. I wish I knew how to change this, how to move outside of myself, but it seems too big to me now. I have built a whole world inside myself. A whole world.

I keep driving.

I try to plan where I will stop. It is night now, and I don't want to drive too late. I want to get past Missoula, and maybe I can get as far as Livingston, where Annie and I stayed before.

I don't quite make it. I had promised my mom I wouldn't drive past dark, but that promise is impossible for me to keep. I told her that to make her feel comfortable; maybe lying is about comfort? We lie to keep things comfortable. There are secrets that are okay to keep, the ones that don't hurt anyone; which lies are those?

I stop for the night in Bozeman. I remember that there are a lot of movie stars who live near Bozeman and Livingston. If my fate had been different I could be neighbors with movie stars. Fate. I made a movie once. I am an actress. I damaged something during this, something I have not yet healed.

The motel where I stay has an indoor pool with a slide; Christian would like this. Kids are running up and down the halls, having fun. Christian is so excited to see me, for me to move there. Annie says he can't wait. It took me a while to get used to having a child, but it was easy with him. He was so loving, so unconditional. We got along great; he could bring me out of myself. Kids have a way of doing this. I remember the first time we went to the beach. It was our first outing. On the way back Christian ate a flower and threw up in his car seat; we had to stop and get paper towels and clean him up. It was then I realized that it wasn't just the two of us. Christian was the other part of this triangle, but I had no faith in how I would handle this. I had never been with kids much, but he was different. He went right to my soul.

In Bozeman, I turn on the Weather Channel to watch the maps. I don't watch Oregon anymore; my attention shifts to Montana, Wyoming, South Dakota — Iowa. Looks like snow in the Black Hills of South Dakota near Sturgis and Rapid City. Iowa looks clear, but still a long ways away. I lie there on some neutral bed with neutral covers and sheets, and I feel alone — alone and free. It is the classic call of motels. It's why Annie likes to have sex in them, the anonymity.

I call Annie to tell her where I am and when to expect me. I feel her doubt again. I think, what have I done? Like when I was twenty-seven and went to Greece. I got off the plane from London at five A.M. and took a cab to the harbor — because all I wanted to do was get to the islands. I stole a thin blanket from the airplane, just in case, and I grabbed a cab. He took me for every cent I had, but I made it to the dock where the boats were waiting. The next boat for the islands left that evening, so I lay on a park bench for eight hours and thought about what kind of journey I had embarked on, what place it would have in my life. I lay there that entire day and thought through the moments of my life, tracing all the steps. I was paralyzed — again. I looked at the people and I saw them see me, but I felt like a ghost. I wanted the world to stop. I wanted to say, "Time out! Stop. Everyone *stop*!" But instead I lay there running the film of my life over and over. Of course it didn't stop, and it was right that I kept moving forward. But in those moments, those moments at the jumping-off point, sometimes there is clarity. I thought of my desire to run, to escape from my problems.

The ferry carried me from Athens across to the islands. I had no sleeping bag, just the blanket that I had stolen from the airplane. I was to sleep on the ferry deck, but my thin blanket did nothing to keep me warm. A woman from Germany asked me if I wanted to share her bag. I crawled inside. She crawled on top of me. We didn't speak; I just looked up at the stars and thought of Sappho while she covered me with her body and slowly moved on top of me.

I found a piece of myself in Greece. At times when I need that piece I can stop and reclaim what I felt when I was there, being in Delphi, looking out over the incredibly lush and green valley. Delphi is called the "womb of civilization." When I stood on her mountains looking out, I could see the mother lying with her legs open, and Delphi was at her center. Her womb. I had gone there to find the woman in the girl. I felt her there. Greece is fertile, and she is green. I was cradled there.

Annie answers the phone. She is nervous. She says her little sister won't come to her house again if I'm there. Her parents won't either. Who then will visit us? Annie went back to be with her family, but her family will reject her life with me. I know how deeply this will hurt her; she tries to be brave but rejection by your tribe is profound.

"I'm just not sure," she says.

I am in Bozeman, halfway there. I can't go back — no, I won't go back.

"Don't be afraid, Annie. Everything will be fine. I can always go home if it doesn't turn out. The road goes both ways." I swallow hard.

She says, "What kind of a commitment is that?"

I had found my comment comforting. I thought she would too.

"I just don't want you to feel trapped." Who don't I want to feel trapped?

After a long pause, as both of us play out our own private movies in our heads, play out different endings in our shared story, she says, "I'm excited for you to come."

This helps.

"Tomorrow night I will crawl in bed next to you." This lightens the moment, but I feel myself panic. If I don't get there quickly something may . . . someone may . . .

I feel her smile. She is warming to me again. I knew she would come around again.

I call my mom. She is not expecting my call. She asked me not to call because she didn't want to wait to hear from me. She and my dad have been watching the news and saw that it is snowing in the mountains. They have been "worried sick" but are glad I called.

"Don't drive before the sun melts the snow in the morning," Mom says.

"I won't," I lie again.

I sleep — but not soundly.

Annie's family has decided I am the cause of her lesbianism, even though she has been in relationships all the way back to when she was fourteen. Her lesbianism precedes mine by seven years, the distance between us. But her parents believe there must be a source, some person responsible for their daughter's life right now. She has returned to persuade them and herself it can all be erased, but I am a confirmation of the secret. Annie knew about herself long before I did. You would think this would make her at ease with it all, and in some ways it does. She is at ease with herself sexually; there is no question this is who she is. She had always believed it was just a matter of deciding not to be. So she moved to Iowa and decided to go straight. But you know, life isn't that easy, and I guess she found this out. She decided if she was going to be with a woman the rest of her life it might as well be me, scars and all.

I wake up, shower, shave everything. This has been our ritual; to shave everything before we see each other. Water. The water washes these thoughts away. I stand there for the longest time and just let the water wash me clean. All my thoughts, gone. *Please go!* I turn my face to the water and wish it was a waterfall. Maybe if I hold my breath and think of movies all will fade from me, but I can't. I keep moving, can't stop. I think about her skin as I shave. She is so soft. She is golden. I think about my mouth on her, her mouth on me. When she makes love to me she is determined.

Her mouth is as accurate as a needle. I have to try hard to hang on as long as possible, to let it linger, but this is hard. I always come too soon.

I dry myself and watch myself in the mirror of the motel. The fluorescent lights reveal everything about me, and I stop for a moment to look at my face. Sometimes when I see myself I don't know who I am, or what I look like. I always expect to see someone else look back. But it isn't *me*. She is another but not me. I used to spend a lot of time in bathrooms when I was little. I would "act" in the mirror, have conversations with myself, dress in my father's clothes. I liked his bathroom because it had his things in it. Shaving cream, deodorant, razors, *Playboy* magazines. I liked the way the women looked back at me. It was their faces and the desire I saw on them that rushed through me. I would make love to dolls, dolls I would fashion out of clothes and wigs and pillows. I would climb on top of them and make love to them, the way I wanted to be made love to. It wasn't as if I was a man; I was me making love to women. I was myself, really, making love to myself.

I choose my clothes for Annie. I wear white. A white long-john shirt underneath a white V-neck T-shirt, Levi's, and brown hiking boots. No makeup. Not until I stop in Sioux Falls, South Dakota, put on makeup, and buy a couple of beers for the last seventy miles. I will crack them open and drink them down as I celebrate the end of the journey. I will toast myself! My courage! The drive!

Tonight I will be in Sioux City.

Tonight.

Annie.

I will see Annie, smell her, taste her, see her smile, look into her beautiful blue eyes. I have bought her many shirts that are light powder blue, for her and for myself, to try and match this blue. But it is unmatched. Tonight I will see her eyes and she will see mine. Blue will meet green with a yellow backdrop of corn and wheat. The hills will spread in front of us, curved like our bodies lying next to each other.

The next morning I make toast at the continental breakfast. The toaster burns one side and doesn't toast the other. I start again and wind up with peanut butter and jelly, milk, and coffee. I take a chocolate doughnut for later and make another peanut butter and jelly sandwich (not toasted) because my card may be denied again.

I am on the road again. Outside it's warm, not too warm but just warm enough. This is a good omen. The movie audience would believe my luck has changed. Weather good. Car okay. Life is good. Memories of the denied credit card dissolve. I may not have much money, but I have enough to reach Annie.

It's still dark out, but since it's warm I'm unconcerned about the roads. At a gas station I wash the mud from my car. This washing is symbolic; it will be contrasted against the washing of my body. A very nice directorial moment here in the film of my life. A ceremonial scene to be included while others are dropped, a scene that reveals something beyond character. Hope against hope must run as a stream through the movie.

I am in Montana, so my foot is heavy on the pedal; there is no speed limit in the daylight. The speedometer reads ninety-five miles an hour. I fly into the "Spiritus Mundi" of the dawn. Are the Faeries out?

At seven thirty-five I am stopped by a policeman.

"In Montana," he tells me, "the sun comes up at seven forty-five. That's ten minutes away."

"How are you supposed to know what time the sun comes up?" I ask.

"If you have to use your lights, the sun isn't up yet," he replies with a smile. I can tell he likes to catch people during "Spiritus Mundi." "I am going to write you a warning." He returns to his car. I watch him in my mirrors. He watches me too. It is seven forty-five when he returns. "Your tags are expired. Did you know this?" I am sure he wishes I were a criminal. Maybe a bomb-carrying white supremacist. Idaho's not far away, after all.

I tell him I am on my way to Iowa. Moving there. Yeah, Iowa. He eyes me. I must look pretty sad with all my belongings piled behind me. He lets me go but reminds me of the subtleties of Montana law. In Montana the sun is on a schedule. I drive under the speed limit until eight-oh-five — just in case.

"Big sky country," Montana. Jesse used to call

Oregon "Big cloud country." The sky is big in Iowa too. Big and everywhere. The sky lies out in front of you like an ocean. And it is blue too. Just like the sea. In the summer there are fireflies, and thunderstorms. When it rains in Iowa it is as if the sea washes the land. Annie's hair is the color of white wheat, the color of the seeds at the top of the stem, the feathers of the stalk. My hair is the color of the light brown rocks at the bottom of the loody. We are the place we come from. Even our bodies are a reflection of that landscape. Annie's eyes are the light blue skies of an Iowa spring; mine are the same as the deep green algae in the tide pools of the Oregon coast.

When the boat finally came to pick us up in Athens, I was ready. I had no cash, just a Visa card with plenty of room on it. I met people on the ferry immediately, including the girl from Germany who took me under her wing and under her body. When the sun came up I could see the island of Lesbos. I stood by the railing, breathing in the islands. I had heard the stories in my theater history classes, so I could recall the mythology of the place. I imagined I would find Sappho here. I was on a pilgrimage.

I met a man on the ferry as we both looked out at the islands. His name was David, and he looked like Michelangelo's. We stayed together on the island for a few days, then traveled around on a motorbike and met a man and his daughter who had a mesquite farm in an olive grove. They lived in a tent and burned the mesquite to sell. They did this in huge mounds of dirt, like giant molehills. Living off the red soil, with nothing but a tent to protect them, a self-reliant man he was. Our dependence on the world seemed silly and superficial as we watched him and his daughter truly live. It was hot there, and their skin was covered with soot. His daughter looked at me with intense interest, but she wouldn't or couldn't speak. This was her life, here on an island, burning mesquite for charcoal. She had one doll, which was covered with soot too, but she held her tightly. Our nomadic spirits must have seemed odd to people so rooted in the earth. David and I slept together under the olive trees with the smell of mesquite burning.

When David came to the United States after I returned home, he looked me up in Portland, but I wanted to keep the memory pure. I had been trying to prove to myself, after Angela, another girlfriend, that I could be with a man, that it was a choice after all. Angela was a phase, I'd decided, not an indication of who I was. It was a confusing but freeing time. I could rewrite myself in Greece. I could be who I had been before, not the mixed-up, dependent girl I had been for the last five years with Angela. At twenty-seven, I had lost myself in the roles I was playing, role after role, as long as it was anyone different from me. I had no idea who I was, having lost sight in the maze of exploration I called my life. Because I went through my own period of uncertainty at twenty-seven, I could better understand Annie's. People can be very judgmental; they think life, time, choices are linear, that it's just a constant progression, and for some it is. But for some of us it is a ball of yarn, winding and unwinding. For some of us it is water. It washes off.

I thought about all the people I slept with after Angela left me. I wanted to conquer them all. I was in search of power, of reclaiming my freedom and resurfacing from drowning in love. Lovers would cure this. Sex would cure this. I was searching for some unreal ideal, someone I could not name.

In Greece, a couple I remember vividly picked me up hitchhiking. I had been looking for a secluded beach by a monastery I had heard about. The temperature must have been over a hundred degrees as I hiked the gravel roads of Crete. It was the day before I was to leave, and I had one more place I wanted to explore. They pulled off the road and told me the place didn't exist, but they had a better place if I wanted to go. He was in the military, and at one time they had been stationed in the U.S. They had a baby. His wife cared for the child and watched us as we swam naked in the unbelievably blue water. She was dark skinned, Greek. She hardly spoke, just simply watched me. Instead of taking me back to my villa in the olive trees, they offered their house in town by the harbor so I could get out the next day and head back for London on time. It seemed a great offer. How could I refuse? They gathered my things and took me home with them.

After dinner, I asked to use their shower. As I stood naked in the bathtub she came in and asked if she could bathe me. I smiled and said yes. I stood and watched her as she bathed every inch of me, carefully, slowly. She took her time letting the water drip from her cloth, lifting my arms, washing my feet, my face, my hair, my breasts, between my legs. I felt sad for her somehow, as if this moment was a dream for her. I let her touch me everywhere; to be touched felt good. It seemed that this was enough for her, but I felt as if I hovered above us, watching. I closed my eyes and let the warm water and this silent, dark-haired woman wash me.

The next morning they took me to the ferry and I took a picture of them with their baby waving good-bye.

Good-bye.

When I got back to London and my hotel room, I lay in the tub and shaved my entire body, peeling a layer of myself away. I had not shaved the whole time I was gone. Maybe it was the layer I had not been ready to give up until then, but with this shave a change happened in me. I knew I had changed. The wild, reckless girl that I had been in Greece was gone. I suddenly desperately wanted something more. I was ready to return to Angela and make a commitment to her. We had continued writing and calling each other for the three months I was gone. Promises made . . .

But when I got off the plane and entered her apartment, too much time had passed. We were too different, and there was nothing holding us to each other anymore.

When I was in Greece I was trying to make a connection with someone, or with myself. Looking for another to fill this hole I swam around inside of. Is this what Annie thinks too? She must. Sex does give you some power back; it is tangible. The power you lose is hard to detect — plus, it takes time to feel the drain.

At Timothy Lake near Mount Hood, Annie and I would hike in and set up camp right on the lip of the lake. At night we took our clothes off and swam in the cool, soft, clean water. The moon bobbed on the water like a dandelion. We would smile and tempt each other in the dark, playing at scaring each other. The coolness took my breath away, that and the touch of her body in the dark water.

A daydream that takes me all the way through to Sundance: *If things don't work out in Iowa, I'll come back through Wyoming and stay in Sundance. I have no money, but I'll find a job as a bartender immediately. I'll continue writing and find a little house way out in the country to live in. I'll model myself after Georgia O'Keeffe, painting, writing, and soaking in the desert sky.* It's good to have a backup plan.

* * * * *

The roads are the worst through Rapid City, South Dakota. I usually stop at the giant drugstore in Wall to buy something — postcard, pen, bumper sticker — to get a good dose of Americana. I don't stop this time. I just want to get there. I still have over three hundred miles in front of me, lots of straight nothingness ahead.

At last I cross the Missouri, my own River Styx. No one to ferry me across this river. A threshold has been reached.

Mitchell's Corn Palace is just ahead. Someday I will stop ... I think about calling Annie, but maybe the anticipation is better, or maybe I'm just afraid to hear her apprehension again. I am either running to her or away from something. Which is which doesn't seem to matter. I knocked myself out for the last two years trying to prove I was worthy, that I was someone you could "hang your hat on," but I don't think anyone could hang a hat on me. Annie thought I was strong and stable too. We fooled each other. We keep wanting each other's true colors to surface, the ones we can both see, the ones we know are there. But this wait becomes a standoff, each of us too proud and stubborn to bend to the other's will. Someday nothing will stand between us; I will see her eyes like I did that first night and she will see me — pure again.

* * * * *

I stop at a little market right outside of Sioux Falls. It is time for my beer! Sioux Falls is the turning point to Sioux City. You turn right. Right in everything. Politics, economics, and religion. All of which I am pretty far left of. The store has a big Midwest woman at the counter who looks like a dyke — but a lot of Midwest women look like dykes. I move past her; my destination is the restroom. I take my makeup in, stand in front of the mirror, and apply some final touches. I am always aware of how I look for Annie. She is so beautiful I want her to see and feel the same attraction for me that I feel for her, but I know she wavers on this. A little girl comes in and stares at me. This is clearly odd for her — a woman putting on makeup in a public restroom. Maybe this is not done in the Midwest? One more reason I don't fit. She can't take her eyes off me, and the good Midwest mother pretends not to notice.

I smile at the little girl. I want to say something like "Yeah, I can't believe it either. Putting on makeup in the middle of the frozen cornfields for a woman who left me six months ago! Now I've chased her halfway across the country to make her love me. So she will know I'm the one. The one who would die for her, the one who stuck it out even when she pushed me away with all her might, all her will. The one who's been chasing God's will back to Iowa — back to the cradle of her parents' thought. Back to the beliefs and lifestyle she was raised to believe in. Raised to believe was right — against what God has created inside of her. Yes, I'm a bit crazy because Annie has to come to this, not me. I can't make her see me. I can't take away fear and hatred of this life — of my love. But here I am, painting my face to lure her back to me. If I look good enough she will have no doubts. All women do this, not just straight ones. Do you see this way of life is not an escape from how we're taught? I'm here hoping to be enough to fill someone's void so as to fill my own, and so it goes . . ."

She smiles back as if to tell me, in her vast wisdom, I am enough. I fail to see this. The movie audience gets it, however. Once again they see the signs that I am oblivious to.

I leave the restroom and shrug to the little girl. She smiles back, and I swear she winks!

I look at the selection of beer — I am not in Portland where there's a good variety to choose from. Rolling Rock is as exotic as it gets, and I want dark. Let it go. The celebratory beer I so looked forward to will have to wait.

My stomach is churning as I travel down I-29 and head for Sioux City, Iowa. I am nervous at what I may — or may not — find. As I get closer I begin to cry. Yes, I am crying as I pull into Sioux City! I don't know why, but I do know I'm not supposed to be crying. Here in Iowa I can't help but feel alone, and the worst part is I can't feel Annie here. She has vanished from me. This whole last week she has vanished. I know I failed to see the signs — chose not to see. I have come on my own accord even when I have felt her gone and unsure. Gone and involved in other things, people, another life.

The countryside looks familiar. The scent of Iowa permeates everything — corn and cows, even in winter.

Sioux City is like a ghost town. Hardly any cars on the streets, I see. What time is it? Nine-fifteen, Monday night, the twenty-ninth of December. I made it in two days! This is a good sign. No cars breaking down — no me breaking down either, unless you count the last thirty miles of tears. The car and I are intact! Quite a lot of worry over nothing, I chide myself. I am ahead of schedule.

The air is cold; the ground is hard. Grass crunches underfoot. God, I'm nervous. I knock, then open the door. She is on the phone with a glass of wine in her hand. She is not as golden as the last time I saw her. She looks beautiful but somehow different. Her eyes are not on fire for me, warm but no fire. They take me for granted.

She hangs up the phone and comes to me. Around her neck is a necklace; as she gets closer I see that it is a silver whale tail on a piece of leather. This is all I see, and my legs feel weak.

She hugs me. "Hi! You made it," she says.

"Yeah I can't believe it." I put my things down.

"What's wrong?" she asks.

"Nothing," I say, but it's clear I am shaken. There is an awkward pause. "Where did you get that necklace?" I finally blurt. I have to ask.

"An antique store." This is a lie. Here we go.

"An antique store in Sioux City?" I don't believe her. She knows this.

"Yes."

"Huh. I like it." I choose to believe. I have to believe.

She smells like garlic. She says she had dinner out with her sister, a place called Minerva's. She had the Caesar salad. She says she told her sister, the one who despises my presence here, that now she will taste of garlic. This was a slip. Her sister looked at her; she understood the reference. Annie laughs and I smile. I tell her I don't mind. She apologizes over and over for this — the garlic.

She takes me through the house. I don't know what she is showing me. All I see is that necklace. She gives me a glass of red wine, and I take a gulp. I need numbness now. What can I hang on to? On her finger I find the ring that I sent her recently. I take her hand in mine as if to remind us both that we are united. I touch the ring; it is real. She catches my eye; I think all is well here. Just my insecurities washing over me. We stand in the kitchen and talk. She comes to me and holds me, then kisses me. I see in her eyes that I have touched something in her, I can see that this comforts her — I know it comforts me. We continue to touch. She continues to kiss me. We go upstairs. I stand over the sleeping Christian.

"He waited for you all day," she says.

He has always been in the middle of us, our complexities and miscommunication. I don't want to wake him. Tomorrow. Tonight I want to be alone with her. I want to find safety and surety in her bed. We take our clothes off — God, she is beautiful . . . I wonder what she thinks of me? We both put on pajamas, I don't know why. I think we are shy. I know I am. I always feel shy with her. It hasn't been too long since we were together, four weeks. We lie on the bed together and take our time. We slowly begin to touch. She is so soft. I lie on top of her; I can feel her strength — she presses hard up against me, wraps her legs around me. We kiss, deeply. I move against her, she moves with me . . . This is good, I remember this. I move down her body. I love Annie's body. It is strong and sensuous. She is feminine yet masculine, and over time she has become more butch. I love this about her, the way she can exude both sides of herself. Her strength and surety come back to me. I put my mouth on her nipples; they are hard like frozen blueberries, and she brings them to my mouth. I leave round, wet circles on her white gauze top. We are naked now. She holds my breasts in her hands, and we laugh. I say she is milking me, too long in Iowa, I say. We laugh softly, continuously. She turns me over and moves on top of me, working her way down my body with her mouth. How long will I last? This is always the hardest part — trying to last — I want her mouth on me for as long as possible. Her lips are thick, swollen. I feel her respond. I have never been with someone who has wanted me in her mouth more than she does; she has a hunger for it. Her mouth finds me — Oh God, her mouth. She is determined as I try to move beneath her mouth. Hang on, I tell myself. Hang on . . . I move my hands through her long, soft hair. I can smell it, I can smell her. I feel her shoulders, her arms, her back. I trace the tattoo on her left shoulder, the cross she bears. I touch her face, her mouth; my fingers find her tongue, and I shadow her movements with my hands. I can see her body, her face, her closed eyes — determined. She is on a mission. I am her goal. I hear her slowly moan as I talk to her. She knows I want her, that she has me in her control. She gets stronger, her mouth sucks harder, and I press myself against her lips. She is gripping me hard, bringing me into her mouth, and as the tears drip from my eyes, she knows how she can have me. She has always been able to have me. When I come my heart is in her hands . . .

She moves back up my body and kisses me. She lies on top of me. I roll her over — I can't wait to taste her. She is clean-shaven, soft. Nothing between my lips and hers. I use my tongue. I like to watch her — she always seems in pain, as if there is much to erase before she can allow herself just to feel. Her mind always seems so full, so heavy with thoughts, from guilt maybe. I have to move my hair out of the way, clear my path. I move her legs apart — I want her open to me. When she comes she breeches — hard. I have to hold on — keep the pressure on. Then all is soft again. We can relax in each other's arms, the tension dissolved. Sometimes when we are together after a long period of time apart, it takes us a few days to reconnect. We mention how this time it's different. How, this time, we move right back into each other.

"It's like we didn't skip a beat," she says. We fall asleep holding each other.

It's like we didn't skip a beat . . .

Early the next morning Christian crawls in between us. He likes to sleep in the middle. He is happy. We hug and I put my arms around him. He reminds me of the time he ate the flower and says that was a long time ago, then he falls asleep.

I can't hear Annie breathing, but she must be awake, I think. I ask her again about the necklace. "Was this a gift?" I ask.

"From him?" she says.

"Yes." I am scared to hear the truth.

"No."

I have to know. "Was it a gift from someone else?"

She pauses. "No."

I remember the ring he gave her, the one with the waves on it, after they spent the night together at the beach, that warm spring day we were supposed to go but fought, the day she felt so guilty she brought me a kitten she found down there; we named her Cannon. She came home — I was helping my niece and her friend with homework — and got angry, went upstairs and cried. I went to her to try and understand what was happening with her, but I couldn't know what she had just done, where she had just been.

Springtime.

I found out too late. They were already on their road together. I was an annoyance to their plans; she tried to forget me and us, but still she couldn't. She thought she found love in him, finally a man — well, a boy — to understand her. Obstacles, yes, but they were "in love."

I don't know what happened — I started to let go, but she couldn't lose me. It wasn't right. He wasn't right. Back to us. Fifteen pounds lighter with a knife through my heart and more baggage than I could carry alone, I took her back and began to try to forget. He and I would not speak again. He had betrayed the truth. *Truth.* The rock I had given him with that word etched on it, but that was a long time ago, before I knew. He drew her a picture of Jesus naked on the cross. She hung it first in our dining room, then above our bed. I tore it in a hundred pieces, after asking his permission. I guess I thought we were still friends somehow, that he was still honest with me.

It was then that things began to change and she started to find her way back to me. But not before they had lied and cheated. His art and words went right to her heart; he knew how to find her but not how to keep her. They tried to make what they had done simple and beautiful and fated. They had captured truth and hung it as Jesus had been hanged. *Truth.* A word with no meaning to them. A shallow attempt at depth, reassurance that their actions were noble because the sum was greater than the parts. They compared themselves to Romeo and Juliet. To me it felt more like a double Judas. You can't make love out of lies. The sting of this betrayal is deeper than any other pain I have ever felt. No two people were any closer to me. She and I had our problems, but I had no idea how deep those problems went. He and I were friends; I was not prepared for his betrayal, and it hit me like a train . . .

My body still reacts like it is happening now, like it is six months ago.

And around her neck hangs a whale tail . . .

I reach across Christian for her hand. I need her reassurance; I am so easily led. I have always believed her even when my insides have called me a fool. But what can you do without proof?

Othello had no proof.

She takes my hand and squeezes it. I let out a sigh. All is good. Why would she take my hand? Why would she want me here? It's just my jealousy and insecurity. When can I trust her again? In time, I will trust her in time . . .

I fall asleep, but my sleep is restless.

In the morning the light is good. Annie gets up right away. No lingering or waking slowly. Christian is awake; he and I linger. We lie in bed, tickle each other and laugh. We smile to each other, feeling blessed. We go downstairs; time for coffee, for establishing our routines. I go to my car for my sack of presents. It was just Christmas, after all. She says that these will be the first gifts they have opened here. We have never spent Christmas together; she has always gone "home" to her family. Maybe now she will see that we are a family. I start my car. It rattles, and there is a high-pitched squeal. I feel lucky, making it here. I will need to fix my car — no rush.

I bring coffee from civilization. Things are good. We open presents; Christian opens his first. I bring him "magic" rocks, candy, seashells for them both to add to their altars of the ocean. His favorite present is the arrowheads I bring him and the pouch to keep them in. For Annie I bought a book on Georgia O'Keeffe; she is enamored of her work. I wanted to frame a picture I painted that was influenced by her work, but it costs too much. I am broke, so instead I bring them treasures from the ocean. I painted a flower for her, a rusty flower surrounded by a green background. In its center is a white light painted over black-speckled seeds. When my mom first saw it she said, "Is that supposed to be the inside of a vagina?"

"Uh, no. No. It's supposed to be a flower," I said.

"Oh. I couldn't tell if it was that or an acorn squash."

So much for painting.

But I do love to paint. It's my newfound "thing." I have been happy with my paintings so far, but more than that I have been happy with the act of painting. I remember my mom used to paint. She would paint in the laundry room. I was always so curious to find her there, painting, alone. I see her now as she sits at her easel, tucked between the washer and the wall, with one small window in front of her — a view of the green wall of the house next door not ten feet away.

Here she painted a world away, a world that was frozen in her mind.

She painted me swinging from the tree on the rope, holding on tight just about to let go. Red-and-blue-striped tank top, jean shorts, and a canvas-and-cloth painter's hat on. Donny, Mark, and me at the loody. Maybe she recognized the specialness of that time, that place, a "Spiritus Mundi." We were the spirits captured in that magic time, captured on canvas as we flew from the cliffs into the green water of the river. Sweet summer fairies. The depth and the smell that were impossible to remember but will never be forgotten. Was there something there she was trying to capture? To keep frozen? She was, after all, the "Queen of the Loody," as we called her. I see the picture of her in a light-colored bathing suit, standing there like a young starlet. Sixteen. Behind her is the tree, the cliff, and the cool summer water of the loody. A prelude to me flying without a cape behind her.

Oils. I can still smell them . . . My mom as painter. This is a mystery to me.

Annie tells me later we will take a ride to see my present. She calls it an investment. My present is an investment. I am reassured. This means a future. This is what I need to hear.

There is a moment sometimes, a tangible moment when everything changes and something happens in someone. Sometimes it is discussed, other times not. Mostly it is a secret only understood by the person to whom it happens. I begin to unpack my car, and this is the moment. I guess it is the moment of realization for Annie that I am here, not on vacation, not for a brief visit, but here. Really here. I see her panic. She is like a small rabbit cornered in a familiar yard by the familiar family pet, but this time the wildness of the rabbit is felt. Will she run? I don't wait to see what she will do. I run, and she makes no effort to catch me.

We go for breakfast. "Too much coffee," she says. On the way to breakfast she talks about Beth.

"I can't wait till you meet her. She's a total dyke." She laughs. "Nothing to worry about. She is not a threat."

She says she feels sorry for Beth. "She has no friends. She needs me as a friend."

I tell her, "I didn't feel other people were threats either, but I was wrong."

She says nothing.

I have no trust in her, no faith in her ability to create boundaries with people. Her need to be needed, to be worshiped by another — like him — is big in her. Alone I can't satisfy this need. It has worn me out trying.

She is silent. We have breakfast. She talks about all the things she and her new friends do. The comment she made a couple of weeks ago about "enjoying being immature" haunts me. She has been on a roll this Christmas vacation. Drinking. Partying. No responsibilities.

Beth was in rehab during high school, Annie says, but "Everyone had a drinking problem." I don't remember that. I was never in rehab. God, who is

she? Has too much time gone by? I see her look at me
like she used to, that look of seeing my age. Seven
years is the road between us. Beth is twenty-six.
Annie is twenty-nine. I am thirty-six. A lifetime apart.
I remember where I was then; I am not there now,
and I know I can't go back. I know Annie wants to
feel weightless, like a balloon. I am like a weight
around her ankles that says *responsibility,* I remind
her that she has entered a new phase in her life. We
see this phase differently now. I know how she feels, I
understand where she is, but I can't change where I
am either. I stay silent. I am not helping things. I
know she is trying to connect to something, but I am
so inside myself now I am gone. I don't know how to
come out because everything we talk about is different
now. She is a new person, not the one I remember.
She has changed. I know I have changed too. I am the
silent, introverted one. I have become so serious and
contemplative. She has moved out of this and is
having fun. God, can I reach her? Can she reach me?
She talks of her friends coming over, picking up where
they left off. I am not part of this. They were four
before, now we are five. This won't work. Whose place
am I taking? Who was taking my place?

She takes me by to see my Christmas present. It is
a beautiful 1950s stereo/console. I am speechless.
When we enter the antique store I look at the jewelry.
"Is this where you got your necklace?" I ask.

"No. It was downtown." Lots left unsaid.

She pays the balance remaining on the stereo.

"I got it for you to play your albums on. I know

you have been looking for one," she says. Proud of her gift to me.

"I sold them all," I tell her.

"That's okay. We'll start over." Again she smiles. That smile that only Annie can smile. The smile that says how innocent she is, how much like a little girl she can be. The smile that says *I love you*. The smile that keeps me here.

As we drive home I notice how silent everything is here. It is like a ghost town. Are we ghosts?

"Are you happy here, Annie?" I ask.

I want her to say, "No. I want to come home. We will. We just have to make it through the year, the winter. It is temporary here." But my life is so temporary. I want to stop. I want a home; I am tired of moving. I want to plant myself somewhere and grow. Annie is still rolling . . . wait. She has stopped, I am still rolling.

"Yes. I am," she says simply.

Silence.

Home again we continue the moving-in process. I bring in the TV and she sits on the couch and begins to cry.

She says, "It's too big. It doesn't fit."

"I know. We can put it upstairs, maybe. Or not. It doesn't matter, Annie. I guess I shouldn't have brought it."

She is crying hard now. "It isn't the TV, Trisha."

I know this. God, how can I not know this.
I stay silent.

"I'm just too stressed right now. I need to go work out or something. The house is . . . it's just too chaotic right now. I can't handle it."

She calls the gym, but it isn't open for another two hours. Two hours.

I put some boxes into the basement; maybe I can set up a desk there, write. I will make a spot for myself there. Back upstairs, I unpack a few books to place on the bookshelf. I watch Annie evaluate them. We have been here before, at this place where my books — my thoughts — become censored. We have discussed this, however; she assured me before I came that this time would be different, but I am finding that nothing is different. I am still a threat to her and her family's beliefs. The books on Buddhism and numerology, *Fear of Flying,* and the gay guide to the U.S. find new homes in the basement. Shoes, clothes, books. Everything in the basement. We will deal with it all later. Man, how do I turn it around! This is not the way I wanted it to be. This is not how I wanted to be. I wanted to "roll with it." But I find I don't roll with much. I understand the panic in her. We have been here before; I know we can weather it. I am beginning to feel in the way. Nothing fits. There is no place for me here. I have to blend in, not be noticed. Disappear. Everything gets worse. The stress.

"This book. Why do you have to put this book up here? If my parents come over they won't understand." She is angry. Which book? I don't even remember now. For God's sake, which book was it? Maybe she feels that she will have to defend me — and herself.

"What's to understand?" I'm angry too. "That people believe different things? That people want to explore different ideas. Maybe, that knowledge is not sinful somehow . . ."

We look at each other. All the old stuff is back. Here we are, and nothing has changed. I say nothing and take the book downstairs.

I know I don't respond well. I feel myself leaving; not only do we live in different worlds, but we like the worlds that we live in. I am silent. The bottom is falling out.

Annie leaves. I am alone. This is what I dreaded, being alone here in Iowa. I am getting angrier now, and I know I will be harder to reach if she tries. I take a shower, make soup, try to feel at home.

Molly and Danielle call.

"How's it going?" they ask.

I can't hide how I feel. "Not too good," I say. "Stressful. Annie's stressed. We just need some time." I act hopeful, but inside I'm not. I hate this. Why is everything we do work? Why does nothing just flow? They're encouraging, but I'm sad. I feel out of place. They don't seem surprised. I tell them Annie wanted them to come by tonight, but they have plans. I'm thinking this would be good, maybe it would help ease the tension. But they seem different to me somehow. Before, we were close, I thought. Now I no longer feel that same bond. Before, they had told me that they were my friends, that if I ever felt lost and alone I could visit them. They helped the last time I came out here, for Annie's birthday. Something in the air then, too, not so obvious though. Her parents had a birthday party for her; they called to tell her I was not welcome there. I was not welcome in their home. I remember the cheese I brought, the cheese that would surely help.

She comes home, but by then I am mad; the tension grows. We are both unreachable. Not even one day here, and she must get away from me. Not good, not good. We eat, play a game with Christian, decide to watch a video. Annie falls asleep immediately. I lie awake with Christian watching *The Sound of Music* until he falls asleep. Annie falls asleep early. I can't wake her up. What is she escaping from? Me.

I carry Christian to bed. I turn everything off, come to bed, and lay my hands on her thigh. She's warm and soft. She doesn't respond. I touch her feet with mine. It's odd. We have always said that this is what we remember about each other, touching each other softly as we sleep. But this time there's nothing. I'm touching her, but she's already gone. I lie awake most of the night. This is the beginning of many nights of sleeplessness for me. I feel her move closer and closer to me throughout the night, and I move closer to her, but neither of us will reach out. She's asleep, that's her excuse. What's mine? I'm not asleep.

I could grab her, hold her. Why can't I reach out for her? I want her to reach for me first, to reassure me that I'm wanted here, that I'm not in the way. I want something she can't give me; she must want something I can't give her. And so it goes . . .

In the morning we have coffee. Avoiding each other's eyes, we sit at breakfast, both of us watching Christian eat.

"We need to talk, Annie," I finally say.

She agrees.

Brief pause. Sound of silverware tapping plates. Christian is silent, then he says, "No fighting."

"It's okay, honey, we're just talking. We won't fight," I say to reassure him.

"I guess I realize I like living alone." Annie sums this all up pretty easily.

I'm stunned. I knew this. We talked about this before I came, but she said she wanted me here, she missed living with me. What can I do now? We haven't even had time to get used to each other again. How can she know this so soon?

"I should leave then," I murmur. It is both a question and an answer. She says nothing.

Just like that.

No response.

Nothing.

This is the end of our communication.

What happened?

* * * * *

"I need to get my car looked at first, then I'll go."

"Your car's fine. It made it here. It was just cold."
Cold. My car is not the only thing that's cold.

She's withdrawn. I know this side of her well, and I know she's somewhere else. I flee so quickly too. I understand. What's there to talk about?

I start to pack. I feel relieved, though, like I have some control back. I'm safe again. I'm taking my life back, putting myself back into a box. I'm protected. I won't be treated like this. I didn't come here to feel like I'm in the way.

"We need to talk to Christian," I say.

"He's fine. It'll just upset him," she replies.

"No, you're fine, Annie. You're fine." I don't know what else to say, so I mumble some ridiculous thing about there not being enough room here for all of us. I know this is wrong. We've always handled this badly. Christian doesn't understand. I don't either. Does she? Christian cries, and I'm so angry and sad . . . We hold each other while Annie keeps her distance. I'm almost packed. She helps put my clothes into the car. Clearly she can't get me out of here fast enough. I begin to cry. Why did I come? "I'll leave today, as soon as I finish packing. No need to wait."

She says nothing.

Instead, she leaves . . . something about errands. She takes Christian with her.

"I'll be gone when you get back . . ." I tell her.

She leaves.

I can't believe this. I heat up some soup to eat,

the soup I made last night. The soup we fought about as I made it. I think of the ring I gave her. It's nowhere to be found; even the box is gone. I think she must have hidden it from me so I couldn't take it, and this gives me hope. Maybe she wants to keep some piece of me, to let me know she still loves me, that she isn't ready for me to go. I look in her jewelery box in the hallway. It isn't there. But I find his. The one she told me she lost, the one we fought over so many times because she continued to wear it after they ended. She said she "liked" it. She didn't understand that the ring made me sick; it was a constant reminder of "them." I'm reminded again of the whale tail necklace. He must've given it to her. The ocean theme is repeated. I go downstairs and in my bag I see the maroon box she'd placed there. The ring is inside with no note, no clue of love, just the last piece of my heart. I break down and cry.

I have no money. How will I make it home? She offers no help. "You'll be fine." This rings true. She's right — I'll be all right. I'm stalling, I don't want to leave — yet something pushes me. She comes back outside to stand by my car. She's been crying but says nothing, just stands there looking at me. Finally she hugs me and says, "Don't hate me."

"I don't, Annie. I know I had to come. You had to see me here, feel me here. We had to know. It just can't work. I guess we know that now. I needed to come. Now we know, now we can get on with our lives." My tone convincing, rational, like this is no big deal — but I'm crying. If she could see inside my body she would see my heart in a puddle, my love screaming for her, but I don't reach out. In some ways I'm already gone. "I'm nervous about driving on a holiday."

Does she remember tonight is New Year's Eve? I don't want to go today, but I want her to ask me to, to say, "Don't leave tonight, go tomorrow. Not tonight. I can't imagine not being with you on New Year's Eve." But she says nothing, *nothing!*

I turn and say good-bye. There's nothing, no recognition in her eyes.

I get in my car.

Wait.

Start the car.

Wait.

Nothing.

I begin to back out of the driveway.

Wait.

I look for her to motion me back inside, if only just to say, "Not yet. You just got here. It's been so long since we've been together, and I just need some time . . . Please give me some time."

Time. Water. Journey. Love. Purpose. God. Jesus. God . . .

"Oh, God, I'm empty. Empty and afraid. I don't want to leave. Please, Annie, please . . ."

But there's nothing, no pause in our fight, no truce for a moment or for a night. She must be in a panic, I think. She has to push me away because she's afraid to have me stay. She's afraid. What's she afraid of?

I leave. No turning back. I'm gone. Just like that. I could turn around, have coffee somewhere, maybe. Lunch. Call later, talk, really talk. I'm running now, too, after so much time — running to think over my life, her place in my life. I need distance. I can still feel the wound of last spring, which hasn't healed; it's not even a scar yet. It's right here, festering. How could I come here with him still looming over us? She wanted me here, she asked me, told me things had changed. This — us, me — was what she wanted. She was ready to make a "commitment." I was leery. She'd wavered twice before, afraid of her family's wrath, their disapproval. She'd gone to Iowa to be near them again, to raise Christian within the circle of their love. I was not a part of her plan, yet here I was. I was afraid of this, and we talked about it, but she was certain. This was what she wanted. But a lesbian daughter and her lover in her parents' backyard was too much. I knew this. It was too much.

I thought I would come here to slay the dragons. I would go into the dark forest and face my fears, face the enemy. But I'm seeing that the dragon is me.

Money — how much money do I have? One hundred and eighty-one dollars, the ATM screen shows. This isn't right, but I feel lucky. The camera peers at the screen over my shoulder. The movie audience senses a change — luck? I have no reason to believe my car will make it, so again I begin to figure where the best place to break down would be.

"I am on an adventure now, no need to worry. I made it this far, I can make it home — sometime. Just like in Greece. I'll make it home. All roads lead home eventually." I must be talking to myself now, out loud at the ATM. Do people talk to themselves in Iowa?

As I wait for the machine to distribute my money, I see Annie and Christian go by. They look like they're on their way somewhere. They don't see me. She isn't even looking for me; she's on her way. She looks happy that I'm gone. Now she can get on with her life. I want to chase them, to get in my car, on my horse, my motorcycle. This would be a great ending for the movie: We embrace. We stumble over "I'm sorry's" while we laugh. We all hug. Aerial shot of us hugging on the deserted streets of Sioux City, Iowa. But no. They're gone too quickly, I can't even stumble my way back to my car in time. If only the light had been red I could have caught them. But wrong movie. Instead I feel embarrassed, stupid for coming. Why didn't I see the signs, or choose to see them? They were before me. But maybe it's like David said: "It's the drive. Sometimes it's just about the drive." God, my whole life has been a drive, and here we go again. I feel like I'm running, like something is pushing me forward, driving me. Maybe it's my angel. Maybe he's saving me or simply dragging me deeper into the forest. I take the ring out of the maroon box and put it on my finger. I make the inscription my own: *You and no other.* I will wear this as a reminder to myself. More crying now. I didn't expect this. Things went wrong so quickly. We spiral fast. People said don't go, but they don't know. It all happened so fast, but once it starts tumbling there's no going back. She didn't want me here; she couldn't wait for me to go. What happened?

I see what this trip is. It's to run this movie past me to recognize some lesson. The windshield serves as a screen, the road the film. I am a captive audience, running into myself, watching the mistakes and the missed opportunities over and over. These people and experiences fly past me. Time folded around itself like a circle. These memories still live in me, perhaps they are happening now as I relive them in my mind. Some fade, some grow stronger; you can't know which is which. Somewhere, out in some other dimension — as music, maybe — that memory of life is being lived.

The weather's good. It's cold, but no snow. The first hundred miles are a blur. I finally stop in Chamberlain, South Dakota. Taco Bell. I splurge! I guess I deserve it. Wow! One day, two nights, and it's over. Just like that. Nothing feels real.

But here I am. Some part of it happened. The drive happened, but I never saw Annie, that's it. She was a body there — barely that — but no soul there to touch. Behind the counter two girls sit looking at me. I wonder what they see. Can they tell anything about me? Anything that just happened? The fact that I just drove seventeen hundred miles to spend one day? The state I am in? What state am I in? Two states really — numb and South Dakota.

Eyes swollen from crying. The woman at the counter is older, she may have insight; perhaps she can see right into the middle of me. But all she does is smile and ask me what I want.

It's all surreal. Maybe I have slipped into some movie, someone else's movie. First it's a tragedy, then a comedy. Quick changes. I look to see if she understands, but no. She stands there looking at me, waiting for my answer, and I hastily place my order.

Maybe this is me in twenty years. Maybe I am being given a vision of myself. I could stay here in Chamberlain, South Dakota, work here where no one would know me. No one could find me. But right now all I want is to go home, back to Oregon. My friends, my family, my womb. I want to go to the ocean, smell the sea, get rained on, smell woodstoves burning by the river, see green again. Home. I just want to be home now.

My car is running fine. I guess Annie was right — I was just stalling, hoping for her to ask me to stay. What a joke. She realized she didn't want me there is all. Maybe she never told her parents I was coming. I am going to spend New Year's on the road; that's probably a good thing. Time to think, put my life back into some kind of order, get focused. I keep looking at the ring on my finger — *You and no other.* Why did she return this? She wants no sign of me. I feel free again. Like a load is off my shoulders, like I am taking care of myself for once. I wonder how she is, what she is doing. Does she miss me? New Year's Eve, on the road.

In fifth grade I met a girl who was unlike any girl I had ever met before. Our parents were friends. We had just moved to Corvallis after living on the beach for the first ten years of my life. I never wanted to leave Newport, but my father's new job took us away. I remember my mom bringing me to the girl's house, telling me we would like each other. She was good looking, not girl-like, more like a boy. She was the first girl I met more like myself — a tomboy, I guess. We slept outside on a mattress together; she lay on top of me, a prelude to the woman from Germany on the ferry. We didn't make love; we kissed and touched each other as we slept outside on the mattress on her patio. We never talked about it. It never happened again, although I think I had a crush on her the whole time my family lived there. She was an athlete and could beat any boy at any sport. It all seemed unfair that she was a girl and would have to put it all away at some time. Of course that's how I thought then; now I look back and see how things really were. Years later when I went back to visit her, it was tense between us. It was as if we couldn't talk anymore. And then I found out she had been hospitalized with bouts of manic depression or something like that. She ended up in the military, and I never heard of her again. But I think of her often, and understand how misunderstood she was, how she must have battled with herself all those years. And I don't know why some people can accept themselves and others torture themselves their whole lives.

That year I lived in Corvallis — the year after my summer, the summer spent at the loody — was filled with kissing and touching, not me and her, but a whole assortment of boys that she knew. I think we were sexual with everyone else to make up for what we wanted with each other. I wonder how many other young girls do this? It was then I began to feel sexual; it all happened in one year. French kissing, finger banging, sneaking out, sex. It was exciting but unemotional, disconnected. Sex did not evolve out of my feelings for someone; it preceded them.

By the time I got to college I had already been aware of feelings, of crushes, but my relationships had been with boys, and I was confident with myself there. College began to change that. I noticed women, and I noticed them notice me.

One girl invited me over to her house. She used to stare at me in class, and when I caught her looking at me all she would do was smile. She was bold. Her name was Alice; she was a long-bodied dancer. She smiled and laughed easily. My stomach would drop and I would feel sick when I saw her. She invited me over one day after school to rehearse. We sat on her floor, leaning against her bed, and she confessed her attraction for other women; she smiled confidently as she told me this. Then she asked to give me a back rub. I lay on my stomach, so nervous I was quivering. I couldn't speak. I shut my eyes, paralyzed, hoping she would know what to do. I couldn't be the one. She touched my breasts, then laid her naked chest on my back. Alice touched my breasts and kissed my neck while her boyfriend worked on his car right outside the door, ten feet from where we lay.

Years later I was living in L.A. and having breakfast at the IHOP on Sunset Boulevard after an all-night session of tequila shots with David and Sydney when I ran into her. She was married. I wonder what she thinks about? I wonder if she remembers herself then? I have thought about her off and on, like some unrealized event. I would have liked to go back there with what I know now, no fear.

I once believed that something had me go to Iowa to face the enemy. I still feel that "something" guiding my life, a force. I am trying to make sense out of the whole thing — this life. God, I wish I could remember it now. That quote. Something about our source being hidden. We just roll along like a river . . . like a car down a highway . . . I remember thinking when I was little that with so many billions upon billions of stars, what if we each had our own star that guided us, that lit our way? God as our own personal star . . . We actually live on the edge of our universe, nowhere near the center. Living on the edge, like the coast.

Balancing on the edge of a dying star's tiny universe . . . How could we possibly be alone?

In Vivian I stop for gas. It's warm out — so warm. Beautiful!

"Our little dying star is pretty warm today." I say this out loud as I stretch at the gas pump with a smile on my face.

The late-afternoon prairie air is almost balmy. It's about sixty degrees on December 31 in Vivian, South Dakota! The people are friendly here, and I actually think about stopping and celebrating the New Year. It seems as if people have already begun to gather. I know people are gathering everywhere — already putting together the game plan — where they will be and who with as the clock strikes midnight. People celebrating the passing of time, like notches on a bedpost. Odd, what we celebrate. Beginnings and endings.

"I guess I should be celebrating our ending, Annie. Maybe you're celebrating a beginning with a new little star. Oh, Annie . . ." Her plans didn't seem to include me. There was something unfinished that I walked into too early. I know her. I know she wouldn't choose to be alone on New Year's. She has someone. I block it out. What's the point?

I went to what I understood — women who liked men but wanted other women. I guess I'm still attracted to this; I understand this.

* * * * *

The roads are clear, the sky cloudless, the wind still. Soon I will be in Wyoming, then Montana — I will sleep in Montana tonight.

The ball of yarn unwinds like this road and keeps circling around itself. And I keep driving. If I drive forever maybe I can find a black hole, drive into it, and make it back to my self that floats around out there in the universe looking for that lost piece, that lost little loody girl.

Rapid City. Sturgis. I always stop in Sturgis, home of the famous Harley rally. Someday I will ride through here on a motorcycle, fast, my hair like a cape. At the convenience store I nuke a meat pocket I took from Annie's freezer. After I finish it I still have no idea what I ate. Meat, yes, but what kind of meat? The warm food feels good in my stomach. I think about the soup I brought to eat, the soup I made at Annie's before I left. But it would only make me sad to eat it now, and I wish I hadn't taken it. I will have a Tupperware container that will take me back, like the coin Christopher Reeve finds in his pocket in *Somewhere in Time*. Suddenly I will be transported back. I will be looking for something to put leftovers in, maybe after a meal with my new lover, and Annie will appear to me. Who will I be then? Where will Annie be? If I could grab a string and vibrate into the future I would know. I would like to know me then. I know that I took it only to have a piece from Annie's house, to prove that I was there. I assume Tupperware will last; it must. I know it will surely outlive me — and Annie.

The roads are the worst here. Some chunks of ice are scattered on the highway, but it's not too dangerous. I stop at a gas-mart. I buy milk and chile cheese Fritos. No holding back now. I feel lucky. I have enough money to make it and if I don't, oh well. A good-looking guy behind the counter asks me what I am doing traveling on New Year's. I tell him it's good to be on the road, "new beginnings." He agrees.

I say, "It's better to be alone than with someone you don't want to be with."

For some reason, I want him to think this solo journey is my idea. Even to a stranger I have to keep the mask on. Clearly this hits him somewhere deep. He looks at me for a moment and stops. "That's right. I know that feeling." And he does, I can tell. Two floating stars have bumped and recognized each other for a brief moment. Here in our little world in the bigger galaxy in a huge universe . . . two have understood.

He wishes me a happy New Year, I wish him the same, and this time we mean it. I wonder what his plans are. A wife? He won't be alone. He and his love will watch the sun rise across the Wyoming moonscape. Maybe they will sit in his convertible with the top down, a sleeping bag wrapped around them — far away from everything, saying nothing, watching the sky, resting their heads against each other, gently falling asleep. As the sun rises they will have made promises that are engraved in their flesh, imprinted with each other's name, like a tattoo. Two parallel lines meeting in infinity.

New Year's has always been a letdown. I remember one. A double date with a crush in high school. We sat in the front seat of some guy's truck with tumblers of rum and Coke looking for the best place to be as the clock struck twelve. How many times has this happened? On the road looking for the best place to be? Instead the other girl and I found ourselves in a gas station restroom at twelve o'clock with two guys that would leave absolutely no trace of memory inside of me. We innocently kissed and said, "Happy New Year." I remember her; does she remember me?

The sun is setting and the Wyoming skies are incredible! Snow is on the ground, the hills, the road, all around me. I wonder how far I will make it tonight. I think of Dean again and how he once said, "Trisha, if you were a city, you would be Missoula, Montana."

To him I was the land and the plains and the mountains and the rivers that are Montana. He placed me here a long time ago. Jesse placed me here too. She made it true because she was Montana. Maybe I tried to steal what was her essence and make it my own — become her because I was unknown to myself. The actress in me would support that. I have done that for so long — assuming identities, shedding skins, becoming someone else. In film you must live the other; onstage you can still move in and out of the identities. When I saw Jesse walk into that restaurant for our first meeting, she was a character right out of a book. She was a railroad conductor with dirty blonde hair she wore in a braid that went all the way to her butt. Her sad hazel eyes revealed a history of having been beaten down by fathers, brothers — men, women, and life.

Montana. I feel at home here and wonder if I should just stop, like in my daydream. But my spirit won't stop; I keep going. I look around and wish that Jesse could have been enough. Born in Anchorage, raised in Kalispell, Montana, she worked on the railroad out of Greybull, Wyoming, after many other starts and stops. I told her when I met her she was like some mythical character. She loved to hear that. I think of the time we took a road trip together — we went up through Montana, down to one of my family reunions, then on to Wyoming. She brought me to a place along the river where there were hot springs. We drove my '76 Volvo across a rickety bridge, found the hot springs where an old building used to be on the river, and swam naked in the warm rushing water. She used to love to show me things. She always wanted to make love to me up behind her old house in Kalispell, up where she and her first love at ten rode horses, escaping the world below, and made love. Jesse never wanted to leave the country, but she knew she had to, to work, to live, to love. All the gay people I have known have had to leave their homes and families to be themselves. It seems so many I know have come from small rural towns and always wished they could return with their love in hand. Annie wished this, for us to live and love in Sioux City. I guess everyone wants to go home. I was young and unsure of still so many things with Jesse; something was missing here for both of us, the life we wanted to live. I always wanted more — or something else. We wanted different things. She wanted to live away from people in the country; I wanted that too, but something more. I wasn't that settled yet. I couldn't stop, just stop and — be. I wish we were friends now, but we don't talk.

Driving across Wyoming on New Year's Eve is lonely. I keep expecting to break down somewhere. There are no cars, no people out on this night. I am all alone here, me and the stars splayed all the way across the skies of Wyoming and southeastern Montana. Time feels so cyclical, like the moon and the stars and the seasons. I could be in New York or Greece or London and I would see the same sky and know these same things.

Wolves. I think of the wolves in the Portland Zoo. They have that faraway, haunted look. What do they think of in their cages, in their pens? They can't run anymore. Annie and I went to the Omaha Zoo once and there was a cage with a female tiger in it. A small cage that she could probably turn around in and nothing more. We got right up close to her and looked into her eyes. They were half alive. I'll never forget that look. I have seen that same look in people. Living in a shell of a body and a shell of a life.

Jesse had no confusion about her sexuality, and her certainty calmed my uncertainty. She was what and who I needed to make that next jump. I needed to name myself. She helped name me. But instead of finding myself, I think I just assumed Jesse's identity, anything to keep me occupied. Jesse and I had a great time at first. It was a long-distance relationship because of her work with the railroad, yet we were close enough to see each other regularly. She was living in Seattle, and I was in Portland, going to graduate school and working as an actress. We told each other we were going to take our time — not become physical until we really knew each other — but Jesse was persistent and not long after we met I got a drunken phone call to meet her. I did and we ended up at a motel. From then on we spent the first year in a lot of motels, since she was always on the road. Everyone liked Jesse. She was fun, had a great personality, and was beautiful — you couldn't help but like her. She carried around with her the scars of an abusive childhood and this made her hard to be around, especially when she drank. Five years later we finally ended it after much hurt and betrayal — this time by me.

Last New Year's Eve, Annie had just come back from Iowa. We went to some party in Portland. The people had a woodstove burning on their porch, and we stood by the warm fire all night, holding each other so close. We looked out over the city, the mountain, the cold clear night. We watched fireworks explode somewhere; the porch creaked beneath our weight. Her smell, sweet and bitter, the wood burning, the green world around us . . . God, some moments hang like fog forever. I remember we were inseparable that night. We stayed close and whispered to each other all the vows we could think of. I promised to follow her to the ends of the earth, or Iowa. She promised never to leave me again. I guess we both lied. Maybe we just didn't know what we were capable of. We kissed outside on the porch, glued to each other, so no one else could penetrate us. Hanging on like we were afraid the world would finally make its way between us. Maybe we were scared. I can see now that she had reason. My reason wasn't as clear, just general fear. Knowing we had already been penetrated. This was the beginning of a bad year; neither one of us knew at that time how bad. But looking back on it now, I wish I could erase most of it, all the bad times that won't let me go.

"You're gone, Annie, but I'm still here, trying to put this all into a place that makes it okay." I wish I could erase the bad times. Don't we all wish we could erase the bad times? "Am I getting mine now, Annie?"

I have learned that anyone can say anything and mean it from a thousand miles away — from two miles away. Lies run deep. I have told my share. Truth is hard come by. Annie's secrets wash across my heart, like a wave. My heart is sad again.

When I left Jesse for Nicole, I too did it over the phone from miles away. I was not courageous. I lied too. I believed that this new person could make me happy, complete. Fairy tales tell us someone will come along and make all our dreams come true. I believed that Nicole could do that. We seemed to "fit" more than Jesse and me. We were interested in the same types of things, we had the same goals, we held many of the same beliefs. I turned her into my savior, and when she didn't measure up I let her go, but when I let her go I let go of all my dreams. I rolled them up into her and threw the whole thing away like a memory out a window. I let go of my desire to act because I believed acting was the problem. Jesse wanted me to believe this; it made our reunion possible. Her love was more important to me then, and besides, I never believed I could have it all. I have never been able to balance the artist in myself with the desire for a committed relationship.

A few years ago, I had seen an advertisement in the paper for an open audition for a small independent film to be shot on the Oregon coast. A lesbian love story. Angela was at that time working for my agent doing bookings and got me the audition for the film. She found out about the film and submitted me for it, then got me a copy of the script and an audition for Noel, one of the two major roles. After reading it I knew I was much more suited for the other major part, the role of Claire. As soon as I read the script I knew her, I had lived her life — our stories were very similar. Like her I had had addictions, anonymous sex, struggled with allowing someone into my heart, felt misunderstood, felt confident with men sexually but barren emotionally. Like her, I too ultimately wanted a meaningful relationship and did not expect this to come to me as a woman.

Feeling awkward and nervous, I read for the part in a room full of lesbians. Wearing my glasses, I attempted some vague reading of "mysterious therapist woman." I thought it odd that the producer, Nicole, had so many lesbians in the room with her. It seemed excessive, but apparently they were making a documentary about the whole process from beginning to end. This seemed a bit pretentious too.

Nicole, however, intrigued me; she seemed very focused but tightly wound. Serious, like me. I felt a kinship there. She had dark brown eyes that looked right into the middle of you, yet she was distant, preoccupied. I felt almost invisible to her. My reading was uninspired, but I asked to read for Claire. Nicole said okay. My audition for Claire went better, but I don't think I turned any heads there. They had intended to go to L.A. to find Claire. After all, Claire epitomized Southern California. But when they returned, disappointed and somewhat confused, Angela pitched me again, telling Nicole that she should take another look at me. I *was* Claire, she told Nicole. They brought me in again, and this time it all went much better. I made an impact on Nicole—personally, too, I guess.

It took a couple of weeks for them to make their final decisions — every moment I thought about the possibility of my dream actually happening . . . I had felt stagnant and unfulfilled in terms of my art. I didn't know where to go and what to do. I grabbed hold of this chance as if it were my last. I guess inside I had always thought this would happen, this opportunity, and when it came I rode it hard. Desperately.

Nicole and I started talking a lot. She would call me late at night or come to my house to look for clothes to use in the movie. It seemed as though she was turning Claire into me, or me into Claire. We were becoming one . . .

I held secrets inside myself from Jesse. I wanted her gone so the transformation would be complete, but I didn't know how to share this with her. I know Jesse saw all of this and it began to worry her, but I think she trusted me, or she had her own demons demanding her attention. I slipped away, slyly, as a traitor.

I was naive and desperate. Not a good combination.

I felt like Faust. No world at my feet, though. Just my lover's heart. That was my brave offering.

We began rehearsals in Portland. A Parisian model had been cast as Noel, and she looked the part, but after one week of rehearsal it was clear she would not be able to make the language leap that was necessary. In a frenzy they held second auditions, and Karen won the role. Karen and I were acquaintances, and I had always been impressed by her talent, her way. We'd met at a workshop many years ago. In a circle, on the grass by the beach, the two of us bared our souls alongside twenty other actors. It was an exercise "for art," if I recall.

It was crazy over the next few days, with everyone trying to get everything in order so we could go to the beach and begin filming. We had lost *all* of our rehearsal time recasting the lead, so we would have to wing the shoot.

Here is a hole. A hole of silence in this story. Things that cannot be said, left hanging.

But this I can say. I can tell you how overwhelmed I felt. All the anticipation of a lifetime of dreams had been building up inside me for so long, and I believed it was all coming true. Maybe I felt grateful, maybe I felt insecure and wanted help, maybe it just felt nice to be desired after all the problems Jesse and I had had, maybe I thought it was all a fantasy — all of it, and what the hell! I don't know why I lied to Jesse. Sometimes it's nice to hide in someone new, to forget yourself and see yourself romanticized in someone else's eyes — a pretty classic fantasy. People leave one body to explore a new one. Anonymity is so, so attractive. I'm often reminded of this when I think of what has happened between Annie and me. All the times I have been the one on the other side. And I have been there often. I've never been faithful, never, until Annie. Ironic, huh?

Jesse called me that first morning to wish me the best on my first day of shooting. I felt low. I spent the rest of my time justifying and making myself feel better about what I had done. I broke her heart, but my mantra chanted, "It's okay. Something has to be sacrificed."

I offered you up, Jesse. My Electra.

My mother bought me an electric teapot, which I brought to the beach. That first morning I woke at four A.M., plugged it in, and leaned over the pot to grab a cup. Forever tattooed in the soft underside of my right arm is a scar. A steam burn. Water imprinted in my skin. The liquid lie. A reminder of my betrayal. Eight years later I still have that scar. For the rest of the shoot, we had to cover it with makeup, but sometimes you can see the burn. A sign? Maybe.

I guess I set myself up karma-wise for everything that would happen after that. We made the film far too personal. I lost control of my performance. I was not shaping it, I was living it. I lost a piece of myself, and my performance clearly reflected this. The confusion, addictions, angst were all real — Nicole and I were living it all. I guess I lost my soul. Nicole wanted Claire, not me. I wanted someone to save me. In the end we were both disappointed.

Filming was a blur — twenty-one days, sixteen-hour days, filming the first and second takes, memorizing the script right before the shot, throwing away pages of script, cutting scenes right and left, the ending created in the editing room . . . A blur.

I realized something huge then, something that destroyed my dreams. This was a business. Everything I fantasized about art was forgotten. It's a business — that's it.

Nicole and I lived together for a couple of months after that. We turned her house into a Parisian garret and christened each other with new identities. We threw away our old selves, became our movie selves, and lived this new life together, hiding in our garret. I stayed drunk on red wine; she stayed drunk on me.

We moved her bed into the living room in front of the fireplace, listened to Edith Piaf, pretended we had been lovers in Paris at the turn of the century, and kept the lies flowing like the wine. Nicole dressed herself in illusion for me as I did for her, but the lie was hard to maintain. We both wanted the illusion to continue, but when we burned out there was no fire to fuel us.

I fell apart. I would lie awake at night and listen to the trains go by and long to be lying next to Jesse. To be home. But I couldn't return. I had ruined us. Destroyed us. I had been the one. Me.

It began with a lie. And nothing was real after that.

The end of the film and the reality of Jesse's being out of my life were too much. I began spinning then, and in some ways I haven't stopped. I took anti-depressants for almost a year, went to therapy and attempted to put back together those frayed ends of my soul that I had lost. Jesse wanted me back, took me back, but something died between us. The "us" had suffered too much damage. She couldn't really forgive me; I couldn't really forgive myself. I wanted to be trusted again. I wanted her to be able to "hang her hat" on me. But I was still running, hoping that Jesse's dreams could become my own.

I went back to graduate school, this time to become certified as a teacher. Again I dove into my work. It was just different work. I escaped into my books, my papers, my classes — I was unreachable. I always have a hard time ending relationships. I tend to check out emotionally and leave the business of the breakup to someone else. I found a place to live, an apartment by the river, down a dead-end street, and my family helped me move.

Curled up with my candles and my books, I wrote love poems to a woman who was not much more to me than a dream and I pondered the next phase of my life. I knew this one was over. I wasn't sure just how thoroughly I had destroyed myself as an actor, but knew I had some piecin' to do. I loved living there with my two cats, one of which Jesse and I found along the train tracks on our way to Sauvies Island. He was an orphan with half of his lip destroyed from fighting. In our new incarnation as friends, Jesse and I took him to the vet, healed him, and I ended up with him.

And then I met Annie. It was winter, and I was still recovering. It took me nearly a year to open my heart to her. I never really told her how in love I had just been. I don't think she really wanted to know. We were unlike in this way. Annie would just as soon not know; I on the other hand wanted to know too much. She must've known my situation from the beginning, though, because of the distance I kept. Her initial distrust was evident, but she persisted, kept us together, and eventually I responded in kind.

When I went back to acting last year, I knew it would come at a price. I even understood that my relationship with Annie might be the cost, but when Dean asked me to play Nina in *The Seagull* by Anton Chekhov, which he was directing, I had to say yes. I hadn't acted in years, not since the movie and Nicole. I couldn't have felt more excited about a part. I had done a scene from the play in David's workshop when I was nineteen. I thought I understood her then, but only her youth; now I felt I understood all of her — her drive. Nina says it's about "carrying your cross."

I wanted my students and Annie to see me perform in a live production. My students had inspired me to act again after watching and experiencing the theater through their eyes. I was teaching them to cherish the core that is the theater, that is acting. Now I had to teach myself. I had to find my Grail, my purpose.

Teaching at the rural school had been an escape for me. I wanted to rewrite myself there. But not soon after I started, the film came back to haunt me. Somehow my principal found out about it, bought every copy that was at the local video store, talked the owner into never buying another one, and cleanly wiped my other person out of town.

He called me into his office one day, along with my union representative, and handed me a letter. If in any way my work in the film infringed on my ability to teach I would be let go. Of course all of this was very subjective, and I wondered just what *infringed* meant, but the reality of my future there was threatened. I talked to the teachers' union and they said that they had had a case a few years back where a man had been picked up for hiring a prostitute, but he had successfully won his case.

I said, "I didn't commit any crime, least of all a

felony." I guess in their minds there wasn't much difference.

My principal laid it out in a way that made it clear, however. "The notion isn't that you have committed a crime. The notion is that if it impedes your ability to be effective as a teacher you will not be allowed to teach." He spoke about notions a lot. "I think it's best if the film is not mentioned. I would suggest you take it off your résumé."

I didn't. It wasn't my best work, but I wasn't going to lie. I refused to start erasing my history. Ironically, that month a cable channel showed it over and over. I did have to address it with my students, but in the end I knew I didn't fit at that school. It wasn't home.

Montana. Beautiful, strong, and sensual, this land at night as the sun sets is like another planet. The landscape is like pictures of Mars, pink and beige and gold and purple and green. Rocks, hills, bush. There is a dusting of snow, white. How perfect.

I couldn't feel more alien.

Did we ever have a chance, Annie?

I guess we both need to start new.

You are still gone. Someone new, Annie? Someone new to hide in? You are lucky, but I have nowhere to hide. It is just me on this road — deep into the forest, into the ocean, into myself. Slaying the dragon that is me. The enemy I thought I would find in Iowa was with me all along. I have been looking for God in love, God in my art, God in sex — communion with another. But I can't find God when I can't find myself. God is within us like breath and is love. He is my spirit that Dean misses and the soul that you wanted open to you. He is all around me, on this road and in the café. He has been there every step of the journey while I chase him like a dog chases its tail; and still I can't stop running.

I think of all the movies I have seen that show the wandering cowboy alone in the desert. The modern cowboy is still alone. The desert doesn't change, the people don't change, it's all the same time — over time, overlapping. And I think somehow my journey is different, but I know it's the same. Maybe if I had a horse it would all make sense. But in the capsule of my car I feel like an observer of this world, not a participant. Like it's all just a backdrop and I'm just an animated cartoon washing across it.

In Billings I stop at a Motel 6, where I will ring in the New Year.

After greeting the woman at the counter I go to my room and lie there wishing Annie could find me. I am stopped now. I can close my eyes now and dream in private, wondering if maybe my thoughts will close down too.

Nothing. No sound. No sight. Nothing. I am stopped.

Too much silence.

I turn on the Weather Channel, but I don't care so much.

I don't bother with a bath. No one to bathe for.

I don't shave.

I close my eyes and dream about next New Year's when I promise myself I won't be running.

The next morning, driving through Livingston and into Bozeman, I am stunned by the blue sky and the light of the sun hitting the mountains. I couldn't begin to describe it but I thanked God, because I felt God there. I felt a gift from him that told me that I was getting close to home and the sun would light my way. All that had been dark the night before was clear again. Annie remained behind me, a shadow.

I have breakfast in Bozeman, call Sydney and tell her I am safe and getting closer. She has been worried since I called her from Annie's the morning before and told her in a flood of tears I was coming home. She wants to know what happened, and I inaugurate my standard response to this question: "It just wasn't right."

Over steak and eggs, I read the newspaper, regroup a bit, think about the bombardment of thoughts and memories I had been sparring with all day, all night, all my life. I am exhausted by the thoughts, but they keep showering me. I can no longer feel my body. I am only my head — or my eye, as Emerson would say, one with God, with the universe. I feel I have reached another plane of existence, like I am in a black hole of memories and thoughts that are trying to lead me to a realization, the "lesson" learned. But for now I am on my way again.

I have been striving for something undeniable in my life. Searching for this greater purpose that I somehow am failing to see. This lesson I can't seem to get hold of. Every person I have met has been a vehicle for me to understand and move forward finally. But what do I expect to happen? The fog to lift and reveal a good job, a loyal wife, two kids? This is not my life, I explained to my father, who expressed his concern over my life and the choices I have made. I'm not surprised, I understand his concern. He and my mother simply want my happiness, while they watch me immersed in my own exploration, which is a nice way of putting it, since I'm pretty sure their interpretation is decidedly different. I have been struggling with a piece of myself from the very beginning, a piece that is separate from my relationship with them. It's this drive to understand myself sexually, artistically, and spiritually. To become closer to God. Annie confided in me that her inability to commit to someone stems from the fact that she has never been able to keep her commitment to God. Again, I understand this in her. Our souls are on similar journeys, and we are apparently very dependent on each other for resolution, or at least for clarity.

Time goes by faster now, once I hit Idaho, then Spokane. From here it's all downhill. I stop at the rest stop between Spokane and Ritzville. This time I use the restroom, the inside one, the clean one, the one everyone else uses. This scene juxtaposes with the other and reassures my audience; audiences like bookends.

The wind is so strong it makes my ears ring. The high-pitched squeal in my engine grows louder, and when I don't have the radio playing I can hear it inside my car. It makes me nervous — but on New Year's Day what can you do? I'm determined to make it home. My angel has carried me this far, and he will carry me the rest of the way. I know, too, that this journey home has not really begun because I have not yet returned.

The tri-cities. I stop at the cheap gas station in Kennewick, buy a couple of celebratory dark beers and some chips. I'm almost home, or close enough. I have always liked to drink and drive — not a lot, but a couple of beers and some salt-and-vinegar chips and maybe a Baby Ruth is heaven. I used to buy a beer on my way home from school and think about the day as I listened to talk radio or a tape.

I see the Columbia River, strong with whitecaps breaking like white fireflies. When I cross the bridge into Oregon I know I have made it! My car didn't break down; I didn't break down! I'm still in one piece — well, maybe one small piece missing, but I'm home. The whole episode seems like a dream to me — not a nightmare, just a weird dream. I think of the necklace around Annie's neck and wonder what it was, the whale tail.

The Dalles, two more beers, Taco Bell, one more double-layer taco. I sit with my taco on the curb for a couple of minutes and soak in the familiar cool air, then I remember my beer in the car and I am moving again. Hood River, Troutdale. I can see the lights of Portland on the horizon. Is this what Oz looked like to Dorothy? I thought I would find Oz there in Iowa. Right.

RETURN

When I turn the corner onto Sydney and Dean's street, their house appears as if out of a mist, and I can't believe this is where I have come home to. The pavement is wet, but it's not raining. Odd for this time of year. Will they be here? What will I say? I linger in the car for just a moment before I take a deep breath, close my eyes, thank my angel, and leave the cocoon of my car for a place that all around says Annie to me. Here I am, a refugee from Iowa.

Dean and Sydney are expecting me. They have allowed me to come and lick my wounds here, to regroup. I can't go back to my sister's. That place is done for me — too many memories of Annie and too many questions that I can't or won't really answer.

I'm still running, going somewhere new so I don't have to see myself reflected back in my sister. So I come here; it is temporary like my life has become. I'm determined to change this, to create stability in my life — it's my mantra now.

Then I get angry. I have to be angry, otherwise I would be too sad. I bring the same things into Sydney's house that I brought into the motels that I stayed in along the way. I smell home in the night air — wet pavement, wood burning, rivers, water, grass...

I am determined not to speak with Annie again, to get on with my life. How many times have I repeated that?

Dean and Sydney are sweet. They are supportive. We talk of how Annie and I are different. How we want different lives. They remind me of last spring. How she can't be trusted. I hear them, but my heart hurts.

"Ain't fate weird?" What else can I say? We're sprawled in the living room with glasses of wine. I really haven't had a conversation for two days. No transition. They have no idea. I try to keep up, maintain my confidence and strength, but really I want to curl up in a fetal position and cry.

"What happened? God, you guys . . ." *You* is emphasized, but there's no malice in Sydney's voice.

I glance over at her. "I know. I know. It just wasn't right. She wanted me to go."

"Oh, God. She'll call. I can't believe you two."

I know I have to offer some kind of explanation, but Sydney seems content for now with what I say.

She will ask more later. Maybe she's tired. Maybe she senses I need to rest. Maybe she just doesn't know what to say.

I slowly ascend the stairs. I will stay in the blue room.

I shut the door, lie down on the bed, and cry.

I am resigned not to talk with her. She has not called. Good, because I will not talk with her. But isn't she worried if I made it? I could be dead along the highway somewhere, Montana maybe. Maybe I didn't even make it that far, maybe Mitchell, South Dakota. Maybe I am staying near the Corn Palace. Maybe she just doesn't care. It's New Year's Day. Evening. About eight o'clock. What happened?

I'm now beginning to see that something more was going on in Iowa for Annie. My suspicions are haunting me. I want them to be true so I know I'm not crazy but, God, I don't want them to be true. I go to bed. I cry myself to sleep.

On Friday morning I go to work as if nothing has happened. I hardly missed a day. I teach. Sort of. Mostly I'm numb. It's all been a dream. It never really happened...

Everything is so much the same that I feel reality slipping away. Everything except that I am now at Sydney's. Thank God for the blue room.

I come home, and waiting is Dean with a message from Annie. She's angry, can't believe I left. Expected me to return. I didn't. New Year's was fine. She had her party. Her life is unchanged. I imagine she is relieved.

I call her. So much for strength.

I don't remember much until she admits the necklace was a gift from Beth, but they "were not physical before I got there." I guess this is to reassure me. But they have been "physical" now. Of course this is a lie too.

Translation: They were physical before, and now they have continued. I am in Annie-speak now. You have to read between the lines.

My stomach churns, and all my suspicions are true. I don't know what to do, what to say. I'm sick, I'm crying, I'm . . . My legs are gone. I knew this when I walked in — the necklace, the phone call, the dinner out with her "sister." I don't know what to say, what to do. I guess I knew, I knew the minute I walked into her house. No, I knew the night before I left. No, I knew before that, when she spoke of her. They spent far too much time together. She repeated to me over and over, "There is no way; she's not my type. You shouldn't feel at all threatened." And in my heart I knew, my angel knew. Annie tells me I should have stayed, we could have talked about it.

I tell her, "What would we have said? You wouldn't talk to me."

"I was going to commit to you as soon as you got here. She didn't mean anything to me."

But now she confesses she has feelings for her. *Feelings for her.*

Feelings.

I am taken back to Nicole, to Jesse. My phone call, my *feelings,* I lied, like Annie, just like Annie.

She has confessed to Beth that she still has feelings for me.

Feelings — for me.

Four years, six months of hell, not being able to let each other go, loving each other from a distance of nearly seventeen hundred miles, commitments made over the phone. Promises. "This time it will be different. I can do this now. I want you here." Flying out for Thanksgiving, spending time at the beach, reconnecting, finally committing to moving to Iowa. All my fears of the week before, all of the doubts, my friends' warnings. Four years of helping to raise Christian, fighting against ourselves, each other.

Feelings.

I still have feelings for Trisha. The thought of her telling Beth that makes my skin crawl.

I'm crushed. I'm defeated, Annie, you win. You've given me the final blow.

I deserved it all, Annie. Maybe not from you, but from someone. This is how life works. I'm getting mine. Karma.

I'm sorry, Jesse. Now I know. I'm sorry.

Annie's crying, she feels bad. My mind wanders to the beginning, when we were new, when we hid in each other. When we were innocent and in love, deeply, deeply in love . . .

* * * * *

When Annie and I lived in McMinnville she lived on the edge of town. Close by was a man who had lions. At night, especially in the spring and summer, you could hear the lions roar. One night we went to see them. We had been on a daffodil run, collecting flowers to bring home, to fill the house with. We would regularly pick the fresh flowers as they came into bloom. My favorite time was when the lilacs were ready. You had to pick them quick and many, because they turned so fast. But this night was filled with daffodils and lions. The closer we got, the more keen they became. It was clear they could smell us. I felt so sad for them, in their cages; they seemed half alive, like the tiger in the cage at the zoo. Annie and I sat on the hood of the car; it was warm. I wanted to make love to her there, for the lions, for us. She lay back on the hood of the car, and I put my mouth on her. I could smell her, the lions, the daffodils. Warm and wet, ready, she moved inside of my mouth, her clit snug between my lips, held there with my teeth. My hands braced her legs against the hood of the Chevy, the silver-blue car that matched her eyes, the lion's mane that matched her own.

It was this moment, this one moment I will always remember like the rain in Newport. Our spring before we lost it. Our innocence before we lost it. Our love before we spun out of control like twisters through each other's life.

But not now, now you are mine here, and I hang on to you and this moment with you, me, the lions, the daffodils . . . She comes in my mouth. The air is filled with our scents — her scent — and the straw from the lions' cages. The lions' nostrils flare, their eyes look at us like prey; they too have been fed. Her legs glimmer with strands of spiderwebs running the length of her thighs. Like the legs on a glass of fine red wine. My mouth glimmers too; the lions and I have fed. We are all alive again. We lie on the hood of my car, next to each other, eyes to the stars, smiles on our mouths, mine still wet. *You stars, you see us now, you know.* This moment I tuck inside of me, deep.

Maybe when Annie hears lions she thinks of me . . .

I know the drive was something I had to do. Something I had to go through to find some peace, to understand. Annie didn't want me there, I came too early, she was starting something new with someone else. No bad memories. She could be new with her. No guilt here. I reflect too much of what is bad in her. I have known her too well. She doesn't want that person anymore. Beth helps her forget; to Annie she is "wonderful." This is what she told me last spring when she was with him. "He tells me how wonderful I am." I'm the one who shows her the other Annie, the one she hides. The one who refuses to die.

So with Beth she is reborn. Beth gives her space and understanding and doesn't push or ask questions or want answers, or want something in return. Beth is content with Annie's presence in her life. I wanted Annie's soul. And so it goes . . .

I let go as best I can. Remember the drive out there and back, and some of the discoveries I made, but they are all vanishing as I see Annie fade in my life. I am still in love with her; no matter what, my love is still strong for her. But I will try to let her go. I call her friends, the friends that were to be our friends, the friends that couldn't wait until I got there so they would have someone to do things with. Their coldness stings me. Their allegiances have shifted, out of necessity or out of desire I don't know.

They say, "They seem happy. Beth's a nice girl."

They seem happy, they seem happy, they seem happy, they seem happy . . .

It's me who is unhappy. Let go. If Annie is happy, well then, all right. Annie tells me she still wants me. "Why did you leave? Why didn't you stay so we could talk?"

"Annie, can't you see me anymore? How could you think all would be fine with this hanging there between us. You knew I would find out. How did you think I would feel? Why didn't you tell me before I came . . . ?" But I know I needed to make the drive. Maybe Annie needed to see me there . . .

She says she doesn't know, over and over again. She says that when I got there she and Beth would be over, that she was ready to make a commitment to me — this stops me. How do you just decide one day to commit? I should know this kind of "commitment" isn't good. It's forced and represents that dreaded loss of something, freedom, freedom without growth. Keep running, Annie, keep running.

Maybe this was her last hurrah, her final moment of being single, like the guy who has sex with a girl the night before he gets married. It's a very male way of dealing with relationships, seeing commitment as an end, not a beginning. I was coming to her as an end, and Beth still represented her freedom and desire not to be committed, especially to someone who knows her so well. But she's safe from me again so she tells me she still loves me, wants me back, tells me she's sorry . . . I soak this up, this is what we do, our dance. Annie makes a mistake and I forgive. So I forgive and the cycle begins again. I've not returned from anything. I've not learned anything.

God, I wish you could bring me home.

The third time we went to Palm Springs was last spring. We had a hard year. I had just finished the play; I thought maybe we could reconnect. It was too late. She had already connected with someone else. I didn't know it at the time, but there had been some clues that I refused to see. Pictures drawn and given. Time spent talking, carefully hiding their moments. I remember talking with him right before we went to Palm Springs. Something or someone was new in his life; I didn't know it was her. I walked in on them once talking. They sat very, very close, and he was whispering into her ear. They both looked up. It was an uncomfortable moment but I still had no idea — I couldn't imagine. How could they? When we went to Palm Springs he and his girlfriend were going to take care of our dog, Hana. It all seemed so friendly, so innocent. Clear enough now, but like seeing the fog lift in the rearview mirror.

We left for the desert while there was a desert between us. I can't say I blame her for seeking out comfort and intimacy in someone else. I had done the same many times in previous relationships. But other boundaries were broken here, betrayals and lies that carved a canyon inside me that I have not been able to cross over.

In Palm Beach, she dove into crossword puzzles and I dove into correcting papers. We slept together, but something was missing between us. I didn't push it; I was happy to have the space, I guess. I think I felt it was ending too. As soon as school was over we would reevaluate. She spoke of going back to Iowa, living the life she knew was right. She would go straight; I would find someone I could understand, who would understand me, dive back into my work, my books — my students had inspired me. It would be best. But we were still in love, we were still connected in some way we both denied but were drawn to.

I bought her a ring there, a different one, one with a fish on it. She bought a hat with the Chinese symbol for peace on it.

We sat in the hot tub every night and watched Comet Hale-Bopp shoot across the sky. Again we talked about stars, planets, life, life beyond, the future. But we didn't try so hard to connect. We stayed separate, aloof.

The last night we were there she swam naked at night in the pool alone. She asked me to swim with her; I felt too distant, I didn't want to be close — it would be too hard. But I sat in the house and watched her swim. I was envious of the freedom and the sensuality of the swim. I will never forget watching her. I knew then there was someone else on her mind, someone she was hiding very deep. I didn't know who it could be. When we returned we sat in the L.A. airport and wrote a poem together. Once again trying to connect. She was searching for something in me to hang on to; I was floating too high above.

When we returned it all fell apart very fast. The lies, the betrayals, the absolute absurdity of the situation. The confrontations, his loyalties going back and forth like a wild animal. Caught in so many lies, both of us. I wanted to run so far away, but I was caught too. Responsibilities. My pocket full of keys. I wish then I would have flown away, run and not looked back. Taken a drive.

Back to my routine, like I never left. But on Monday when I teach something happens. My stomach heaves, I begin to cry, this is it, I'm losing it. I'm losing it and can't keep myself together. Just like last spring. I wish I was in the womb of my car, driving. I wish Annie would cradle me. I sit in a phone room at some high school, needing to call her, someone. I need someone to call. Maybe him, the one who all this started with, but I can't. I remain loyal to Annie. Talking to him would be a betrayal. Besides, what would I say? Maybe I'm just feeling like I did last spring all over again, and I am just reminded of him. The sick feeling of being at school and knowing they were together. The betrayals all over again. She is always looking for another to fill her. I've never been enough, and I never will be. I need to go home. But I can't. I won't give up! I decide to write and I go to my room and I begin: "The night before I went to Iowa I got scared . . ." And I feel myself heal.

The ball of yarn and time winds around itself, and I feel all the people from my past all rolled up into Annie. Everyone I have loved — Jesse, Nicole, Annie — it's all the same thing. Time travel is possible. I think about what the physicist said, that time travel is possible because all time is happening at the same time; time is not linear. It is cyclical, folding back over itself. I'm still that child at the loody. When I drive, my parents are still sitting next to me in the passenger's seat, Dean and I are still in Eugene . . . I continue to live over the moments of my life in every moment of my present one. My soul going round and round. Faces of all whom I have loved and have run

from, of all who have run from me. I don't blame
Annie. How can I? I have not been there. I have been
running from her from the beginning. She looked for
someone else to fill the void that I left. I pushed her
away with my fears. And she knows how to run too.
She runs to others and I run inside, where I have
always felt safest. The womb of myself.

I will cradle me.

Two months later, I made my last trip to Iowa,
this time to rescue Annie. She had swallowed a
handful of pills and sedatives, then called me. I
opened my heart once again. It had been too long. I
called her parents, told them she was in trouble. I felt
I'd betrayed her.

Later she thanked me. She said, "You love me."

"Yes," I whispered. *Yes.*

It's March. The snows are melting. The road's
clear. I have always believed in Annie's heart, and I
know she has believed in mine, and while we have
hurt each other deeply, we have loved each other. I
don't know anyone anymore whose love, or road, has
been smooth. I know too that many have stayed
faithful from beginning to end and never faltered. I
can't speak to this; this has not been me, and I know
it's not been Annie. I've loved her and she's loved me,

and although she has slept with others and I know I've been distant and afraid, we have weathered something together. Her body's like food to me; she's like water.

In Sioux City she takes me to her favorite haunts. I begin to see her again. I watch her play pool, that slight smile across her face as the simple action of cue against ball against ball into pocket lights her up. We dance together, and again I feel her desire for me, our movement together, apart and together. Her smile exudes want, simple want. Mine returned, even though she refused to talk about the pills. I finally dropped the issue. The point had been made. She was calling for help, and I came. Her body is like a goddess's, strong and golden. When I touch her body I still feel the same charge of warmth and fear. We sleep close and breathe together again.

Christian and I paint. We create a space in the basement and decide this will be our "artistic haven." We paint for Annie's mother, who's in the hospital after having surgery. We paint Christmas trees and red flowers with purple centers. The flowers we paint live in yellow fields where the sky is blue and cloudless. We have a showing in our new gallery of his art. Mine is camouflaged in his. We paint together and tell each other how brilliant we are.

One day in March, Annie, me, and our friends here, Molly and Danielle, took a drive into the countryside of Iowa. They were intent on showing me the "real" Iowa. We bought a case of beer and drove into the rolling hills around Sioux City. Even Hana came along, wagging her tail, anxious to run. As we drove away from town, Molly spoke of what it was like for her living here. How the people make it special, how they treat you as gently as the corn in their fields. She says that in the spring the farmers pick up the soil and press it into their fingers, feeling the moisture in it so they know when it's time to plant. She believes it's these gestures that make the people nurturers; they treat each other like the seeds they plant and watch grow. There're only a few people here, she says, that judge; most are content to live and let live.

We drive by the farm where Danielle lived with her husband, before she left him, before she stopped denying herself and her sexuality. In the process the South Dakota courts took her two boys from her. The sacrifice of wholeness, I guess. We silently drive by the farm out into the snow and the fields and the openness. Around the land the pieces of farm equipment lie like fossils, unused and unprotected. Abandoned. Like this place had been left in a hurry and no one had returned to put the pieces back together. A hawk flew overhead, searching for some small animal to feed on. The farm was still a personal devastation. The framed pictures of her boys hang like spirits in her house; she no longer sees them, but they live with her every day.

We drive through the town of Jefferson, passing by

135

Bud's Bar, Larry's Bar. Molly's dad says that all it takes is a church and a bar to make a town in Iowa. We play in the snow, watch Hana run, and I do see the land like the sea. We drive down these roads here like they're rivers. We laugh about the people we see, and we see the people laugh at us — they want me to see what they see, and I do.

Her mother embraced me one night. She spoke of how the rest of the family still finds it wrong and how she is accused of not being a Christian because she has acknowledged my existence. I see this hurts her, but she too has discovered something. She wants to understand, not necessarily to agree, but to understand. She needs to know what her hand in it was, because she created Annie. Is she responsible for the creation? Not all of it. It's like a flower in a way. You can plant the seed, but you can't know what the life of the flower will be.

She says, "I told them it isn't for me to judge. I can only love and leave the rest up to God. I know he has a plan for us all. But they think because I am nice to you and have you both over that I'm condoning it, that I think it's okay to be gay."

And I don't remember what she said next. I think I was scared to hear those words again — that it's wrong and we are surely going to hell — but she doesn't say that. She's just upset because she too is being judged. Once the tables are turned and God gives us the opportunity to see the other side, to be judged, you're forever changed. No one can know this until you have the experience, but it's true — and I believe truly a gift.

Annie and I get closer daily. But we have changed. Maybe after having so many others in between, we chip away at what was special between us. I know I have lost my confidence with her. I know she has lost her desire for me. I'm too familiar, like that old worn T-shirt I gave her so long ago. Did I know this would come to be me? Maybe in Annie's youth she sees new as exciting. Sex must be always changing, or always fueled with a burn and a charge. Maybe in my age I have discovered something different. What I used to think of as exciting — anonymity and risk — come out of our own fears of intimacy. I remember the movie I was in so long ago and find the irony now in it. In the movie we talked about intimacy, yet truly there was no intimacy experienced. Really it was about conquest and surrender. I have given up on that battle. I was like Claire, like Annie. Now I see I need more, that there's something in the gentleness of love and the small details.

I told Annie to see me as a candle — not brilliant, but warm. Soft. I reminded her that one candle can heat the inside of an entire car.

In the Iowa soil the strong yellow daffodils are surfacing, gasping for breath. On my way home from school one day I stop to buy some for Annie. I will surprise her at school. If I could bring her lions today too, I would. Her car isn't in the school parking lot, so I head home, figuring she's gone home for lunch. At home her car is gone. My heart begins to pound, and I feel myself collapsing under the weight of suspicion. Instinctively I know where she is. I turn my car around and drive to Beth's house. The daffodils lie next to me on the seat, their mouths open. They could be smiling, their stems appear so strong, but inside they are hollow. They drip on my seat. Her Jeep sits in front of Beth's house. I don't stop, I keep on driving by. Instead I go home. I stand in the kitchen with my fingers suffocating the green fragile stalks. I know they need water, I know they need air — but I can't let them go . . .

Annie walks in the house two hours later. Have I been standing in the same place for that long? In my hand I see the yellow, open-mouthed flowers.

"Hi. Oh, where did you get the flowers?" Annie smiles. In her eyes I see she remembers. She seems so relaxed.

"I bought them at the store. I brought them by the school for you at lunch. You were gone." I'm trembling. The flowers are dying in my hands.

"Oh, I went by the store to look at window boxes," she says.

"Which store?" I ask.

"The Coast to Coast store," she says as she puts her bag in the closet. She has turned away from me. I watch her. There is no sign on her body, in her face, that she has lied, that she probably just slept with someone else.

"I saw your car at Beth's. I went by her house."

"Are you checking up on me?"

"Yes," I say. "I just knew. How long has this been going on?" Please just say the truth, Annie. It's pointless to lie anymore.

"This wasn't the first time." She looks me straight in the eye.

I explode. "I fucking hate you! How could you? Not again, not fucking again. I can't go through this again." I storm down to the basement to start packing. Annie follows me down. "Get the fuck out of here! Leave me alone," I scream, the flowers still clenched in my hand. It seems surreal to be feeling what I'm feeling and have these withered flowers captive in my hands. I tear them apart and throw the pieces at her. I pick up my paintings to keep them safe, but she takes them from me and tears them up. She then takes my easel and swings it like a bat against the wall. "Why do you want to destroy me? Why do you hate me?" I scream as I see myself as painter crumbled into a pile in the middle of the basement.

"It isn't you I hate, it's me!" Her anger comes out now like a fierce wave. "I just want to die! All I do is destroy!" Surrounded by my paintings, the easel, and the torn and thirsty daffodils, she falls to the floor and cries. Slowly the anger in me crumbles and I lie with her in the cradle of the house, the two of us entwined like scared kittens. We lie there for a long time, silent, holding each other. Then we make love ... Her eyes stay open to me, and her kisses are long and wet. Her fingers desperately hide inside me, holding on, like my hand around the flowers ... I wish we could stay here forever, like in *Brigadoon,* asleep and entwined for a hundred years. Two sleeping lions on a bed of daffodils.

Leaving the forest, the dark night coming to an end, all of a sudden I realize it's no longer dark, but light. I don't remember when it happened, only that it did. I wonder what the movie audience will see? What will the final image be of this part of the story?

On the snow outside there's white and there's light. The sun is out, and I stand on the hill behind our house watching Hana run and go crazy with something like happiness. She runs through the snow, eating it, mouthfuls of white powder; like a snow plow she runs. I look all around me and all I see is blue open sky. The air is still. I feel my spirit whole for the first time; I don't know why. I do know that whatever happens now, I am okay.

I feel the pieces of myself come together like the continents, an ocean between myself and myself, merging back together after my decade of spinning ... My dream as a prologue to what my life will be. I feel by knowing this now something big has been achieved. No, I'm not a superstar, Dean, I'm not a superhero. But I'm finally myself — whole.

I remember the Emerson quote now: "Man is a stream whose source is hidden." We do roll along like a river, and where we spring from is unknown. And we return to the source, and the source may be hidden as a person or a place. But the source, ultimately, is of God. We can spend our whole lives trying to figure it all out, our journey, our destination, *why*. We just have to trust, like Amiri Baraka says; you just gotta trust your "oom boom ba boom." Emerson calls it nature, the *source*. John Lennon says, "I am the Walrus. Koo koo ka choo." And as one of my first students used to say, "It's all good." You're right. It's all good.

Spring is full now. I can see how this is when Iowa really comes alive and the ugliness I saw before has disappeared and all I see is green. I've never experienced spring like this; I can't believe it's the same place. It's transformed. In all I have read about spring I finally see. The world does change. There is much that has lain beneath the earth, sleeping deathlike, that suddenly appears. Life is amazing ...

We spend time working in the yard, and perhaps the garden we plant is a way of planting something in each other. We work together at this, weeding, planting, watering, shaping. Soon we have brought the dead yard back, and where there was nothing but weeds we now have hope for some flower to surface. Just what will appear neither one of us knows. This is part of the joy, the surprise. But every once in a while we find something new. My mom always said to "leave a place better than when you got there." I carry this with me, trying to leave something better behind me, but I'm afraid I'm running from a place where this may not be so.

The spring changed into summer and so did we — hot and happy, but with the knowledge we would soon end, just as summer would change into fall. Much happened, but we seemed to move into a rhythm together. Underneath it all, though, Annie still needed to attempt the life that called her back. So as the summer slipped away I got a call to return to Portland to teach. I didn't want to go, even though I had reason to believe it would be for the best. Despite everything, I had made her and Christian my home.

The night before I left for Oregon Annie and I lay in bed holding hands as we slept. Again the whole journey ran through my mind, and I didn't wonder where Annie was because she was warm and next to me. The morning was gentle and civil as we calmly packed my life back into the capsule of my car. The rain fell softly — feathery, like Oregon rain, either calling me or taunting me, just like the morning I returned to Iowa. It was a bookend morning, and I guess teachers like bookends. We cried as we carefully worked. Christian told me he would "walk to Oregon to see me." I told him I loved him and when he came to see me I would take him to the beach.

I called Annie's mother to say good-bye, and she asked me an odd question. "Is someone driving you?"

I said, "No. I'm driving alone."

"No, I mean making you go?"

"No," I said.

But the words stuck in my head somewhere as I pulled out of yet another driveway. Her words tapped at my thoughts like the rain against the windshield.

"Driving me . . . ?"

Behind me stood Annie and Christian, Hana at their side. Waving and crying. In my mind the movie of Annie plays out before me. I see her standing in front of me the first time we met. Soft and kind. Her beauty dwarfed by her brighter spirit. I hope I have not dulled her light, the light that brought me to her, her smile that ruled me. I had no strength in the face of her smile. It has never, ever been easy for me to walk away from her. I knew I needed to leave — finally and cleanly without mean words and meaner actions.

Driving me. Again I thought about her mother's words as I drove by the Yankton–Vermillion cutoff. *Driving me.* Well, I suppose someone is, or has been the whole time, although all along I thought it was me. Yes, I felt my angel next to me, but I never thought of myself as the passenger. Maybe what drives me is the same as what drives the movie audience that I have always felt close to. Maybe it's the person I talk to in my head, the one I'm talking to now, the one living inside me. Yes. Someone is driving me. I pulled over to the side of the road and stopped the car. Just stopped. I turned off the engine and watched the rain sweep across the grass like the large hand of

God. I listened to the rain fall. I felt the land soak it in. Again I saw myself as the rain and Annie as the land and I knew I could not feed her. I knew then that home was not a destination but a feeling, and I knew that I would have to make this place for myself, finally and completely. The rain reminded me of who I was and where I needed to return to find her. I started the engine of my car somewhere in South Dakota and drove home.

Months have now gone by. Annie and I kept in touch for a while. She even spoke of possibly returning to Oregon, but that has changed again. She's met a man and is in love with him now. She says she knows this is hard for me to hear, but she wants to be honest now. I have always wanted honesty — truth. I guess I have been in search of that as much as anything. I think Annie is in search too. Truth must come to us as air. We must breathe it. I hope Annie is breathing her truth now. But I miss her . . .

I hear her voice, but the Annie I knew is gone now, has retreated and given herself over to this new person she speaks of now. Instead of her voice I have my own inner dialogue that I hang on to. At odd times during the day — in my car, first thing when I wake up, before I fall asleep, in front of my students — I repeat these words over and over: "I love you. I am sorry." I feel like a child reciting the Jesus prayer. I don't know why, but I find it comforting. But saying

Annie's name places her next to me. I guess the sound of her name, being composed of many strings, takes me to her. We are still tied together. Sometimes I still wish for a wormhole to crawl into and meet Annie at the beginning, or at some time in the future when we are once again in harmony. I know she has nothing to be sorry for. She's just being Annie, trying to make her own way. She's on her own road. God, how well I know that . . . Recently we spoke. Guardedly, like survivors of a plane crash who check in on each other as if to not forget. She told me she's raising butterflies now.

Annie is raising butterflies.

She's rewriting herself.

Transforming herself like a butterfly.

Here's a moment . . . This moment I tuck away.

As I followed the river home into Oregon one warm summer evening, I remembered why it was my home. Why this place is me. The green trees shoot up into the sky, and it's difficult to see any one tree through the thick forest. The river is wide and swift, just like the Missouri. But this river has an ocean at its end.

Sixteen hundred and eighty-two miles away is a sea of corn. I swam in that sea for a while. I didn't drown — here I am — I've surfaced. I smell the loody now. When I need her, she's close. I've come home, and no doubt I will climb up the familiar rocks again. I will stand waiting to jump, and I will fall through the air to the safety of the water below, where I will continue my descent and hold my breath for as long

145

as possible, staying under for as long as possible. Then I will shoot up through the dark cool water, ascending as if to heaven, as if in flight. My spirit is simply the water and the air around me. God is all around me as I float weightlessly toward the inevitable breath I will take. I will remember this moment . . . I cannot help but gasp for air — it's too much in my nature.

Maybe that's how we should always return from the drive. Breathless.

Trisha Todd will sign *The Drive* at Book Expo America. At press time a West Coast tour is planned; a Mid-Western and an Atlantic Coast tour are also likely.

Look for spot interviews in dozens of gay and lesbian media nationwide.

The Drive is featured in the *Independent Reader,* Spring 1999 (LPC Group).

Trisha Todd is the cover feature of the May 1999 *Girlfriends* magazine.

An excerpt of *The Drive* appears in the March 1999 issue of *Curve* magazine.

Read on . . .

Born and raised in Oregon, Trisha Todd received her Bachelor's degree from the University of Oregon, studied theater in London, traveled through Europe, then moved to Los Angeles, where she began her acting career. In 1988, she decided to return to graduate school at the University of Portland and received her M.F.A. in acting and directing in 1990. She then returned to Europe to continue her studies in theater and backpacked by herself through the Greek islands for two months.

Shortly thereafter, she was cast as the nubile Claire in the popular lesbian film *Claire of the Moon* (1992). Well-versed in theater as well as film, Todd has also played the roles of Desdemona in *Othello,* Nina in *The Seagull* and Stella in *A Streetcar Named Desire.*

Her lifelong love of school and books then led her to teaching, and in 1993 she began to teach drama and English just outside of Portland, Oregon. In 1995, wanderlust struck again. "I put all my things in storage, bought a van, traveled across the country and began a year of exploration that resulted in this book," she says. Now living in Portland, she teaches at an inner-city school and spends her free time writing, reading, and studying the classics and mythology, her passions. Future plans include continuing her writing and returning to acting.

LOOKING FOR NAIAD?

Buy our books at
www.naiadpress.com

or call our toll-free number
1-800-533-1973

or by fax (24 hours a day)
1-850-539-9731

THE DRIVE by Trisha Todd. 176 pp. The star of *Claire of the
Moon* tells all!   ISBN 1-56280-237-2 $11.95

BOTH SIDES by Saxon Bennett. 240 pp. A community of
women falling in and out of love.   ISBN 1-56280-236-4   11.95

WATERMARK by Karin Kallmaker. 256 pp. One burning
question . . . how to lead her back to love? ISBN 1-56280-235-6   11.95

THE OTHER WOMAN by Ann O'Leary. 240 pp. Her roguish
way draws women like a magnet.   ISBN 1-56280-234-8   11.95

SILVER THREADS by Lyn Denison.208 pp. Finding her way
back to love . . .   ISBN 1-56280-231-3   11.95

CHIMNEY ROCK BLUES by Janet McClellan. 224 pp. 4th Tru
North mystery.   ISBN 1-56280-233-X   11.95

OMAHA'S BELL by Penny Hayes. 208 pp. Orphaned Keeley
Delaney woos the lovely Prudence Morris.   ISBN 1-56280-232-1   11.95

SIXTH SENSE by Kate Calloway. 224 pp. 6th Cassidy James
mystery.   ISBN 1-56280-228-3   11.95

DAWN OF THE DANCE by Marianne K. Martin. 224 pp. A dance
with an old friend, nothing more . . . yeah! ISBN 1-56280-229-1   11.95

WEDDING BELL BLUES by Julia Watts. 240 pp. Love, family,
and a recipe for success.   ISBN 1-56280-230-5   11.95

THOSE WHO WAIT by Peggy J. Herring. 160 pp. Two
sisters . . . in love with the same woman. ISBN 1-56280-223-2   11.95

WHISPERS IN THE WIND by Frankie J. Jones. 192 pp. "If you
don't want this," she whispered, "all you have to say is 'stop.' "
                                      ISBN 1-56280-226-7   11.95

WHEN SOME BODY DISAPPEARS by Therese Szymanski.
192 pp. 3rd Brett Higgins mystery.   ISBN 1-56280-227-5   11.95

THE WAY LIFE SHOULD BE by Diana Braund. 240 pp. Which
one will teach her the true meaning of love? ISBN 1-56280-221-6   11.95

UNTIL THE END by Kaye Davis. 256pp. 3rd Maris Middleton
mystery.   ISBN 1-56280-222-4   11.95

FIFTH WHEEL by Kate Calloway. 224 pp. 5th Cassidy James
mystery.   ISBN 1-56280-218-6   11.95

JUST YESTERDAY by Linda Hill. 176 pp. Reliving all the
passion of yesterday.   ISBN 1-56280-219-4   11.95

THE TOUCH OF YOUR HAND edited by Barbara Grier and
Christine Cassidy. 304 pp. Erotic love stories by Naiad Press
authors.   ISBN 1-56280-220-8   14.95

WINDROW GARDEN by Janet McClellan. 192 pp. They discover
a passion they never dreamed possible.   ISBN 1-56280-216-X   11.95

PAST DUE by Claire McNab. 224 pp. 10th Carol Ashton
mystery.   ISBN 1-56280-217-8   11.95

CHRISTABEL by Laura Adams. 224 pp. Two captive hearts and
the passion that will set them free.   ISBN 1-56280-214-3   11.95

PRIVATE PASSIONS by Laura DeHart Young. 192 pp. An
unforgettable new portrait of lesbian love . . .   ISBN 1-56280-215-1   11.95

BAD MOON RISING by Barbara Johnson. 208 pp. 2nd Colleen
Fitzgerald mystery.   ISBN 1-56280-211-9   11.95

RIVER QUAY by Janet McClellan. 208 pp. 3rd Tru North
mystery.   ISBN 1-56280-212-7   11.95

ENDLESS LOVE by Lisa Shapiro. 272 pp. To believe, once
again, that love can be forever.   ISBN 1-56280-213-5   11.95

FALLEN FROM GRACE by Pat Welch. 256 pp. 6th Helen Black
mystery.   ISBN 1-56280-209-7   11.95

THE NAKED EYE by Catherine Ennis. 208 pp. Her lover in the
camera's eye . . .   ISBN 1-56280-210-0   11.95

OVER THE LINE by Tracey Richardson. 176 pp. 2nd Stevie
Houston mystery.   ISBN 1-56280-202-X   11.95

JULIA'S SONG by Ann O'Leary. 208 pp. Strangely
disturbing . . . strangely exciting.   ISBN 1-56280-197-X   11.95

LOVE IN THE BALANCE by Marianne K. Martin. 256 pp.
Weighing the costs of love . . .   ISBN 1-56280-199-6   11.95

PIECE OF MY HEART by Julia Watts. 208 pp. All the
stuff that dreams are made of —   ISBN 1-56280-206-2   11.95

MAKING UP FOR LOST TIME by Karin Kallmaker. 240 pp.
Nobody does it better . . .   ISBN 1-56280-196-1   11.95

GOLD FEVER by Lyn Denison. 224 pp. By author of *Dream
Lover*.   ISBN 1-56280-201-1   11.95

WHEN THE DEAD SPEAK by Therese Szymanski. 224 pp. 2nd
Brett Higgins mystery.   ISBN 1-56280-198-8   11.95

FOURTH DOWN by Kate Calloway. 240 pp. 4th Cassidy James
mystery.   ISBN 1-56280-205-4   11.95

A MOMENT'S INDISCRETION by Peggy J. Herring. 176 pp.
There's a fine line between love and lust . . .   ISBN 1-56280-194-5   11.95

CITY LIGHTS/COUNTRY CANDLES by Penny Hayes. 208 pp.
About the women she has known . . .   ISBN 1-56280-195-3   11.95

POSSESSIONS by Kaye Davis. 240 pp. 2nd Maris Middleton
mystery.   ISBN 1-56280-192-9   11.95

A QUESTION OF LOVE by Saxon Bennett. 208 pp. Every
woman is granted one great love.   ISBN 1-56280-205-4   11.95

RHYTHM TIDE by Frankie J. Jones. 160 pp.   . . . to desire
passionately and be passionately desired.   ISBN 1-56280-189-9   11.95

PENN VALLEY PHOENIX by Janet McClellan. 208 pp. 2nd
Tru North Mystery.   ISBN 1-56280-200-3   11.95

BY RESERVATION ONLY by Jackie Calhoun. 240 pp. A
chance for true happiness.   ISBN 1-56280-191-0   11.95

OLD BLACK MAGIC by Jaye Maiman. 272 pp. 9th Robin
Miller mystery.   ISBN 1-56280-175-9   11.95

LEGACY OF LOVE by Marianne K. Martin. 240 pp. Women
will do anything for her . . .   ISBN 1-56280-184-8   11.95

LETTING GO by Ann O'Leary. 160 pp. Laura, at 39, in love
with 23-year-old Kate.   ISBN 1-56280-183-X   11.95

LADY BE GOOD edited by Barbara Grier and Christine Cassidy.
288 pp. Erotic stories by Naiad Press authors.   ISBN 1-56280-180-5   14.95

CHAIN LETTER by Claire McNab. 288 pp. 9th Carol Ashton
mystery.   ISBN 1-56280-181-3   11.95

NIGHT VISION by Laura Adams. 256 pp. Erotic fantasy romance
by "famous" author.   ISBN 1-56280-182-1   11.95

SEA TO SHINING SEA by Lisa Shapiro. 256 pp. Unable to resist
the raging passion . . .   ISBN 1-56280-177-5   11.95

THIRD DEGREE by Kate Calloway. 224 pp. 3rd Cassidy James
mystery.   ISBN 1-56280-185-6   11.95

WHEN THE DANCING STOPS by Therese Szymanski. 272 pp.
1st Brett Higgins mystery.   ISBN 1-56280-186-4   11.95

PHASES OF THE MOON by Julia Watts. 192 pp. . . . . . hungry
for everything life has to offer.   ISBN 1-56280-176-7   11.95

BABY IT'S COLD by Jaye Maiman. 256 pp. 5th Robin Miller
mystery.   ISBN 1-56280-156-2   10.95

CLASS REUNION by Linda Hill. 176 pp. The girl from her
past . . .   ISBN 1-56280-178-3   11.95

DREAM LOVER by Lyn Denison. 224 pp. A soft, sensuous,
romantic fantasy.   ISBN 1-56280-173-1   11.95

FORTY LOVE by Diana Simmonds. 288 pp. Joyous, heart-
warming romance.   ISBN 1-56280-171-6   11.95

IN THE MOOD by Robbi Sommers. 160 pp. The queen of
erotic tension!   ISBN 1-56280-172-4   11.95

SWIMMING CAT COVE by Lauren Douglas. 192 pp. 2nd
Allison O'Neil Mystery.   ISBN 1-56280-168-6   11.95

THE LOVING LESBIAN by Claire McNab and Sharon Gedan.
240 pp. Explore the experiences that make lesbian love unique.
                                         ISBN 1-56280-169-4   14.95

COURTED by Celia Cohen. 160 pp. Sparkling romantic
encounter.   ISBN 1-56280-166-X   11.95

SEASONS OF THE HEART by Jackie Calhoun. 240 pp. Romance
through the years.   ISBN 1-56280-167-8   11.95

K. C. BOMBER by Janet McClellan. 208 pp. 1st Tru North
mystery.   ISBN 1-56280-157-0   11.95

LAST RITES by Tracey Richardson. 192 pp. 1st Stevie Houston
mystery.   ISBN 1-56280-164-3   11.95

EMBRACE IN MOTION by Karin Kallmaker. 256 pp. A whirlwind
love affair.   ISBN 1-56280-165-1   11.95

HOT CHECK by Peggy J. Herring. 192 pp. Will workaholic Alice
fall for guitarist Ricky?   ISBN 1-56280-163-5   11.95

OLD TIES by Saxon Bennett. 176 pp. Can Cleo surrender to a
passionate new love?   ISBN 1-56280-159-7   11.95

LOVE ON THE LINE by Laura DeHart Young. 176 pp. Will Stef
win Kay's heart?   ISBN 1-56280-162-7   11.95

DEVIL'S LEG CROSSING by Kaye Davis. 192 pp. 1st Maris
Middleton mystery.   ISBN 1-56280-158-9   11.95

COSTA BRAVA by Marta Balletbo Coll. 144 pp. Read the book,
see the movie!   ISBN 1-56280-153-8   11.95

MEETING MAGDALENE & OTHER STORIES by
Marilyn Freeman. 144 pp. Read the book, see the movie!
                                         ISBN 1-56280-170-8   11.95

SECOND FIDDLE by Kate 208 pp. 2nd P.I. Cassidy James
mystery.   ISBN 1-56280-169-6   11.95

LAUREL by Isabel Miller. 128 pp. By the author of the beloved
Patience and Sarah.   ISBN 1-56280-146-5   10.95

LOVE OR MONEY by Jackie Calhoun. 240 pp. The romance of
real life.   ISBN 1-56280-147-3   10.95

SMOKE AND MIRRORS by Pat Welch. 224 pp. 5th Helen Black
Mystery.   ISBN 1-56280-143-0   10.95

DANCING IN THE DARK edited by Barbara Grier & Christine
Cassidy. 272 pp. Erotic love stories by Naiad Press authors.
ISBN 1-56280-144-9   14.95

TIME AND TIME AGAIN by Catherine Ennis. 176 pp. Passionate
love affair.   ISBN 1-56280-145-7   10.95

PAXTON COURT by Diane Salvatore. 256 pp. Erotic and wickedly
funny contemporary tale about the business of learning to live
together.   ISBN 1-56280-114-7   10.95

INNER CIRCLE by Claire McNab. 208 pp. 8th Carol Ashton
Mystery.   ISBN 1-56280-135-X   11.95

LESBIAN SEX: AN ORAL HISTORY by Susan Johnson.
240 pp. Need we say more?   ISBN 1-56280-142-2   14.95

WILD THINGS by Karin Kallmaker. 240 pp. By the undisputed
mistress of lesbian romance.   ISBN 1-56280-139-2   11.95

THE GIRL NEXT DOOR by Mindy Kaplan. 208 pp. Just what
you d expect.   ISBN 1-56280-140-6   11.95

NOW AND THEN by Penny Hayes. 240 pp. Romance on the
westward journey.   ISBN 1-56280-121-X   11.95

HEART ON FIRE by Diana Simmonds. 176 pp. The romantic and
erotic rival of *Curious Wine*.   ISBN 1-56280-152-X   11.95

DEATH AT LAVENDER BAY by Lauren Wright Douglas. 208 pp.
1st Allison O'Neil Mystery.   ISBN 1-56280-085-X   11.95

YES I SAID YES I WILL by Judith McDaniel. 272 pp. Hot
romance by famous author.   ISBN 1-56280-138-4   11.95

FORBIDDEN FIRES by Margaret C. Anderson. Edited by Mathilda
Hills. 176 pp. Famous author's "unpublished" Lesbian romance.
ISBN 1-56280-123-6   21.95

SIDE TRACKS by Teresa Stores. 160 pp. Gender-bending
Lesbians on the road.   ISBN 1-56280-122-8   10.95

WILDWOOD FLOWERS by Julia Watts. 208 pp. Hilarious and
heart-warming tale of true love.   ISBN 1-56280-127-9   10.95

NEVER SAY NEVER by Linda Hill. 224 pp. Rule #1: Never get
involved with . . .   ISBN 1-56280-126-0   11.95

THE WISH LIST by Saxon Bennett. 192 pp. Romance through
the years.   ISBN 1-56280-125-2   10.95

OUT OF THE NIGHT by Kris Bruyer. 192 pp. Spine-tingling
thriller.   ISBN 1-56280-120-1   10.95

LOVE'S HARVEST by Peggy J. Herring. 176 pp. by the author of
Once More With Feeling.   ISBN 1-56280-117-1   10.95

FAMILY SECRETS by Laura DeHart Young. 208 pp. Enthralling
romance and suspense.   ISBN 1-56280-119-8   10.95

INLAND PASSAGE by Jane Rule. 288 pp. Tales exploring conventional & unconventional relationships.   ISBN 0-930044-56-8   10.95

DOUBLE BLUFF by Claire McNab. 208 pp. 7th Carol Ashton Mystery.   ISBN 1-56280-096-5   10.95

BAR GIRLS by Lauran Hoffman. 176 pp. See the movie, read the book!   ISBN 1-56280-115-5   10.95

THE FIRST TIME EVER edited by Barbara Grier & Christine Cassidy. 272 pp. Love stories by Naiad Press authors.   ISBN 1-56280-086-8   14.95

MISS PETTIBONE AND MISS McGRAW by Brenda Weathers. 208 pp. A charming ghostly love story.   ISBN 1-56280-151-1   10.95

CHANGES by Jackie Calhoun. 208 pp. Involved romance and relationships.   ISBN 1-56280-083-3   10.95

FAIR PLAY by Rose Beecham. 256 pp. An Amanda Valentine Mystery.   ISBN 1-56280-081-7   10.95

PAYBACK by Celia Cohen. 176 pp. A gripping thriller of romance, revenge and betrayal.   ISBN 1-56280-084-1   10.95

THE BEACH AFFAIR by Barbara Johnson. 224 pp. Sizzling summer romance/mystery/intrigue.   ISBN 1-56280-090-6   10.95

GETTING THERE by Robbi Sommers. 192 pp. Nobody does it like Robbi!   ISBN 1-56280-099-X   10.95

FINAL CUT by Lisa Haddock. 208 pp. 2nd Carmen Ramirez Mystery.   ISBN 1-56280-088-4   10.95

FLASHPOINT by Katherine V. Forrest. 256 pp. A Lesbian blockbuster!   ISBN 1-56280-079-5   10.95

CLAIRE OF THE MOON by Nicole Conn. Audio Book — Read by Marianne Hyatt.   ISBN 1-56280-113-9   16.95

FOR LOVE AND FOR LIFE: INTIMATE PORTRAITS OF LESBIAN COUPLES by Susan Johnson. 224 pp.   ISBN 1-56280-091-4   14.95

DEVOTION by Mindy Kaplan. 192 pp. See the movie — read the book!   ISBN 1-56280-093-0   10.95

SOMEONE TO WATCH by Jaye Maiman. 272 pp. 4th Robin Miller Mystery.   ISBN 1-56280-095-7   10.95

GREENER THAN GRASS by Jennifer Fulton. 208 pp. A young woman — a stranger in her bed.   ISBN 1-56280-092-2   10.95

TRAVELS WITH DIANA HUNTER by Regine Sands. Erotic lesbian romp. Audio Book (2 cassettes)   ISBN 1-56280-107-4   16.95

CABIN FEVER by Carol Schmidt. 256 pp. Sizzling suspense and passion.   ISBN 1-56280-089-1   10.95

THERE WILL BE NO GOODBYES by Laura DeHart Young. 192 pp. Romantic love, strength, and friendship.   ISBN 1-56280-103-1   10.95

KATHLEEN O'DONALD by Penny Hayes. 256 pp. Rose and
Kathleen find each other and employment in 1909 NYC.
ISBN 1-56280-070-1   9.95

STAYING HOME by Elisabeth Nonas. 256 pp. Molly and Alix
want a baby . . . or do they?   ISBN 1-56280-076-0   10.95

TRUE LOVE by Jennifer Fulton. 240 pp. Six lesbians searching
for love in all the "right" places.   ISBN 1-56280-035-3   11.95

KEEPING SECRETS by Penny Mickelbury. 208 pp. 1st Gianna
Maglione Mystery.   ISBN 1-56280-052-3   9.95

THE ROMANTIC NAIAD edited by Katherine V. Forrest &
Barbara Grier. 336 pp. Love stories by Naiad Press authors.
ISBN 1-56280-054-X   14.95

UNDER MY SKIN by Jaye Maiman. 336 pp. 3rd Robin Miller
Mystery.   ISBN 1-56280-049-3.   11.95

CAR POOL by Karin Kallmaker. 272pp. Lesbians on wheels
and then some!   ISBN 1-56280-048-5   11.95

NOT TELLING MOTHER: STORIES FROM A LIFE by Diane
Salvatore. 176 pp. Her 3rd novel.   ISBN 1-56280-044-2   9.95

GOBLIN MARKET by Lauren Wright Douglas. 240pp. 5th Caitlin
Reece Mystery.   ISBN 1-56280-047-7   10.95

FRIENDS AND LOVERS by Jackie Calhoun. 224 pp. Mid-
western Lesbian lives and loves.   ISBN 1-56280-041-8   11.95

BEHIND CLOSED DOORS by Robbi Sommers. 192 pp. Hot,
erotic short stories.   ISBN 1-56280-039-6   11.95

CLAIRE OF THE MOON by Nicole Conn. 192 pp. See the
movie — read the book!   ISBN 1-56280-038-8   11.95

SILENT HEART by Claire McNab. 192 pp. Exotic Lesbian
romance.   ISBN 1-56280-036-1   11.95

THE SPY IN QUESTION by Amanda Kyle Williams. 256 pp.
A Madison McGuire Mystery.   ISBN 1-56280-037-X   9.95

SAVING GRACE by Jennifer Fulton. 240 pp. Adventure and
romantic entanglement.   ISBN 1-56280-051-5   11.95

CURIOUS WINE by Katherine V. Forrest. 176 pp. Tenth Anniver-
sary Edition. The most popular contemporary Lesbian love story.
ISBN 1-56280-053-1   11.95
    Audio Book (2 cassettes)   ISBN 1-56280-105-8   16.95

CHAUTAUQUA by Catherine Ennis. 192 pp. Exciting, romantic
adventure.   ISBN 1-56280-032-9   9.95

A PROPER BURIAL by Pat Welch. 192 pp. 3rd Helen Black
Mystery.   ISBN 1-56280-033-7   9.95

SILVERLAKE HEAT: A Novel of Suspense by Carol Schmidt.
240 pp. Rhonda is as hot as Laney's dreams.   ISBN 1-56280-031-0   9.95

LOVE, ZENA BETH by Diane Salvatore. 224 pp. The most talked
about lesbian novel of the nineties!   ISBN 1-56280-030-2   10.95

A DOORYARD FULL OF FLOWERS by Isabel Miller. 160 pp.
Stories incl. 2 sequels to *Patience and Sarah.*   ISBN 1-56280-029-9   9.95

MURDER BY TRADITION by Katherine V. Forrest. 288 pp. 4th
Kate Delafield Mystery.   ISBN 1-56280-002-7   11.95

THE EROTIC NAIAD edited by Katherine V. Forrest & Barbara
Grier. 224 pp. Love stories by Naiad Press authors.
    ISBN 1-56280-026-4   14.95

DEAD CERTAIN by Claire McNab. 224 pp. 5th Carol Ashton
Mystery.   ISBN 1-56280-027-2   9.95

CRAZY FOR LOVING by Jaye Maiman. 320 pp. 2nd Robin Miller
Mystery.   ISBN 1-56280-025-6   11.95

UNCERTAIN COMPANIONS by Robbi Sommers. 204 pp.
Steamy, erotic novel.   ISBN 1-56280-017-5   11.95

A TIGER'S HEART by Lauren W. Douglas. 240 pp. 4th Caitlin
Reece Mystery.   ISBN 1-56280-018-3   9.95

PAPERBACK ROMANCE by Karin Kallmaker. 256 pp. A
delicious romance.   ISBN 1-56280-019-1   10.95

THE LAVENDER HOUSE MURDER by Nikki Baker. 224 pp.
2nd Virginia Kelly Mystery.   ISBN 1-56280-012-4   9.95

PASSION BAY by Jennifer Fulton. 224 pp. Passionate romance,
virgin beaches, tropical skies.   ISBN 1-56280-028-0   10.95

STICKS AND STONES by Jackie Calhoun. 208 pp. Contemporary
lesbian lives and loves.   ISBN 1-56280-020-5   9.95
Audio Book (2 cassettes)   ISBN 1-56280-106-6   16.95

UNDER THE SOUTHERN CROSS by Claire McNab. 192 pp.
Romantic nights Down Under.   ISBN 1-56280-011-6   11.95

GRASSY FLATS by Penny Hayes. 256 pp. Lesbian romance in
the '30s.   ISBN 1-56280-010-8   9.95

THE END OF APRIL by Penny Sumner. 240 pp. 1st Victoria
Cross Mystery.   ISBN 1-56280-007-8   8.95

KISS AND TELL by Robbi Sommers. 192 pp. Scorching stories
by the author of *Pleasures.*   ISBN 1-56280-005-1   11.95

STILL WATERS by Pat Welch. 208 pp. 2nd Helen Black Mystery.
    ISBN 0-941483-97-5   9.95

TO LOVE AGAIN by Evelyn Kennedy. 208 pp. Wildly romantic
love story.   ISBN 0-941483-85-1   11.95

IN THE GAME by Nikki Baker. 192 pp. 1st Virginia Kelly
Mystery.   ISBN 1-56280-004-3   9.95

STRANDED by Camarin Grae. 320 pp. Entertaining, riveting
adventure.   ISBN 0-941483-99-1   9.95

THE DAUGHTERS OF ARTEMIS by Lauren Wright Douglas.
240 pp. 3rd Caitlin Reece Mystery. ISBN 0-941483-95-9 9.95

CLEARWATER by Catherine Ennis. 176 pp. Romantic secrets
of a small Louisiana town. ISBN 0-941483-65-7 8.95

THE HALLELUJAH MURDERS by Dorothy Tell. 176 pp. 2nd
Poppy Dillworth Mystery. ISBN 0-941483-88-6 8.95

BENEDICTION by Diane Salvatore. 272 pp. Striking, contemporary romantic novel. ISBN 0-941483-90-8 11.95

COP OUT by Claire McNab. 208 pp. 4th Carol Ashton Mystery.
ISBN 0-941483-84-3 10.95

THE BEVERLY MALIBU by Katherine V. Forrest. 288 pp. 3rd
Kate Delafield Mystery. ISBN 0-941483-48-7 11.95

THE PROVIDENCE FILE by Amanda Kyle Williams. 256 pp.
A Madison McGuire Mystery. ISBN 0-941483-92-4 8.95

I LEFT MY HEART by Jaye Maiman. 320 pp. 1st Robin Miller
Mystery. ISBN 0-941483-72-X 11.95

THE PRICE OF SALT by Patricia Highsmith (writing as Claire
Morgan). 288 pp. Classic lesbian novel, first issued in 1952 . . .
acknowledged by its author under her own, very famous, name.
ISBN 1-56280-003-5 11.95

SIDE BY SIDE by Isabel Miller. 256 pp. From beloved author of
Patience and Sarah. ISBN 0-941483-77-0 10.95

STAYING POWER: LONG TERM LESBIAN COUPLES by
Susan E. Johnson. 352 pp. Joys of coupledom. ISBN 0-941-483-75-4 14.95

SLICK by Camarin Grae. 304 pp. Exotic, erotic adventure.
ISBN 0-941483-74-6 9.95

NINTH LIFE by Lauren Wright Douglas. 256 pp. 2nd Caitlin
Reece Mystery. ISBN 0-941483-50-9 9.95

PLAYERS by Robbi Sommers. 192 pp. Sizzling, erotic novel.
ISBN 0-941483-73-8 9.95

MURDER AT RED ROOK RANCH by Dorothy Tell. 224 pp.
1st Poppy Dillworth Mystery. ISBN 0-941483-80-0 8.95

A ROOM FULL OF WOMEN by Elisabeth Nonas. 256 pp.
Contemporary Lesbian lives. ISBN 0-941483-69-X 9.95

THEME FOR DIVERSE INSTRUMENTS by Jane Rule. 208 pp.
Powerful romantic lesbian stories. ISBN 0-941483-63-0 8.95

CLUB 12 by Amanda Kyle Williams. 288 pp. Espionage thriller
featuring a lesbian agent! ISBN 0-941483-64-9 9.95

DEATH DOWN UNDER by Claire McNab. 240 pp. 3rd Carol
Ashton Mystery. ISBN 0-941483-39-8 10.95

MONTANA FEATHERS by Penny Hayes. 256 pp. Vivian and
Elizabeth find love in frontier Montana. ISBN 0-941483-61-4 9.95

THERE'S SOMETHING I'VE BEEN MEANING TO TELL YOU
Ed. by Loralee MacPike. 288 pp. Gay men and lesbians coming out
to their children.   ISBN 0-941483-44-4   9.95

LIFTING BELLY by Gertrude Stein. Ed. by Rebecca Mark. 104 pp.
Erotic poetry.   ISBN 0-941483-51-7   10.95

AFTER THE FIRE by Jane Rule. 256 pp. Warm, human novel by
this incomparable author.   ISBN 0-941483-45-2   8.95

PLEASURES by Robbi Sommers. 204 pp. Unprecedented
eroticism.   ISBN 0-941483-49-5   11.95

EDGEWISE by Camarin Grae. 372 pp. Spellbinding
adventure.   ISBN 0-941483-19-3   9.95

FATAL REUNION by Claire McNab. 224 pp. 2nd Carol Ashton
Mystery.   ISBN 0-941483-40-1   11.95

IN EVERY PORT by Karin Kallmaker. 228 pp. Jessica's sexy,
adventuresome travels.   ISBN 0-941483-37-7   11.95

OF LOVE AND GLORY by Evelyn Kennedy. 192 pp. Exciting
WWII romance.   ISBN 0-941483-32-0   10.95

CLICKING STONES by Nancy Tyler Glenn. 288 pp. Love
transcending time.   ISBN 0-941483-31-2   9.95

SOUTH OF THE LINE by Catherine Ennis. 216 pp. Civil War
adventure.   ISBN 0-941483-29-0   8.95

WOMAN PLUS WOMAN by Dolores Klaich. 300 pp. Supurb
Lesbian overview.   ISBN 0-941483-28-2   9.95

THE FINER GRAIN by Denise Ohio. 216 pp. Brilliant young
college lesbian novel.   ISBN 0-941483-11-8   8.95

LESSONS IN MURDER by Claire McNab. 216 pp. 1st Carol Ashton
Mystery.   ISBN 0-941483-14-2   11.95

YELLOWTHROAT by Penny Hayes. 240 pp. Margarita, bandit,
kidnaps Julia.   ISBN 0-941483-10-X   8.95

SAPPHISTRY: THE BOOK OF LESBIAN SEXUALITY by
Pat Califia. 3d edition, revised. 208 pp.   ISBN 0-941483-24-X   12.95

CHERISHED LOVE by Evelyn Kennedy. 192 pp. Erotic Lesbian
love story.   ISBN 0-941483-08-8   11.95

THE SECRET IN THE BIRD by Camarin Grae. 312 pp. Striking,
psychological suspense novel.   ISBN 0-941483-05-3   8.95

TO THE LIGHTNING by Catherine Ennis. 208 pp. Romantic
Lesbian `Robinson Crusoe adventure.   ISBN 0-941483-06-1   8.95

DREAMS AND SWORDS by Katherine V. Forrest. 192 pp.
Romantic, erotic, imaginative stories.   ISBN 0-941483-03-7   11.95

MEMORY BOARD by Jane Rule. 336 pp. Memorable novel
about an aging Lesbian couple.   ISBN 0-941483-02-9   12.95

THE ALWAYS ANONYMOUS BEAST by Lauren Wright Douglas.
224 pp. 1st Caitlin Reece Mystery.   ISBN 0-941483-04-5   8.95

MURDER AT THE NIGHTWOOD BAR by Katherine V. Forrest.
240 pp. 2nd Kate Delafield Mystery.   ISBN 0-930044-92-4   11.95

WINGED DANCER by Camarin Grae. 228 pp. Erotic Lesbian
adventure story.   ISBN 0-930044-88-6   8.95

PAZ by Camarin Grae. 336 pp. Romantic Lesbian adventurer
with the power to change the world.   ISBN 0-930044-89-4   8.95

SOUL SNATCHER by Camarin Grae. 224 pp. A puzzle, an
adventure, a mystery — Lesbian romance.   ISBN 0-930044-90-8   8.95

THE LOVE OF GOOD WOMEN by Isabel Miller. 224 pp.
Long-awaited new novel by the author of the beloved *Patience
and Sarah*.   ISBN 0-930044-81-9   8.95

THE LONG TRAIL by Penny Hayes. 248 pp. Vivid adventures
of two women in love in the old west.   ISBN 0-930044-76-2   8.95

AN EMERGENCE OF GREEN by Katherine V. Forrest. 288
pp. Powerful novel of sexual discovery.   ISBN 0-930044-69-X   11.95

DESERT OF THE HEART by Jane Rule. 224 pp. A classic;
basis for the movie *Desert Hearts*.   ISBN 0-930044-73-8   10.95

SEX VARIANT WOMEN IN LITERATURE by Jeannette
Howard Foster. 448 pp. Literary history.   ISBN 0-930044-65-7   8.95

A HOT-EYED MODERATE by Jane Rule. 252 pp. Hard-hitting
essays on gay life; writing; art.   ISBN 0-930044-57-6   7.95

AMATEUR CITY by Katherine V. Forrest. 224 pp. 1st Kate
Delafield Mystery.   ISBN 0-930044-55-X   10.95

THE SOPHIE HOROWITZ STORY by Sarah Schulman. 176 pp.
Engaging novel of madcap intrigue.   ISBN 0-930044-54-1   7.95

THE YOUNG IN ONE ANOTHER'S ARMS by Jane Rule.
224 pp. Classic Jane Rule.   ISBN 0-930044-53-3   9.95

AGAINST THE SEASON by Jane Rule. 224 pp. Luminous,
complex novel of interrelationships.   ISBN 0-930044-48-7   8.95

LOVERS IN THE PRESENT AFTERNOON by Kathleen Fleming.
288 pp. A novel about recovery and growth. ISBN 0-930044-46-0   8.95

THIS IS NOT FOR YOU by Jane Rule. 284 pp. A letter to a
beloved is also an intricate novel.   ISBN 0-930044-25-8   8.95

These are just a few of the many Naiad Press titles — we are the oldest and largest lesbian/feminist publishing company in the world. We also offer an enormous selection of lesbian video products. Please request a complete catalog. We offer personal service; we encourage and welcome direct mail orders from individuals who have limited access to bookstores carrying our publications.